THE YELLOW WALLPAPER

AND OTHER STORIES OF LIBERATION

First Warbler Press Edition 2021

First publications:
"The Yellow Wallpaper" in *The New England Magazine*, 1892 | "Why I Wrote the
Yellow Wallpaper" in *The Forerunner,* 1913 | "The Two Offers" in two installments in
Anglo-African, 1859 | "The Prescription" in Harper's *New Monthly Magazine*, 1864 |
"The Story of an Hour" originally published as "The Dream of an Hour" in *Vogue*, 1894
| "The Reckoning" in *Harper's Magazine*, 1902 | "Mrs. Spring Fragrance" in *Hampton's
Magazine,* 1910 | "Miss Furr and Miss Skeene" in *Geography and Plays* (Boston: The
Four Seas Press, 1922) | "What Do You See, Madam?" in *All-Story Cavalier Weekly*,
1915) | "Sweat" in *Fire!!*, 1926 | "Sanctuary" in *The Forum,* 1930

Introduction and Author Biographies © 2021 Ulrich Baer

ISBN 978-1-954525-83-2 (paperback)
ISBN 978-1-954525-84-9 (e-book)

warblerpress.com

Printed in the United States of America. This edition is printed with
chlorine-free ink on acid-free interior paper made from 30% post-consumer
waste recycled material.

THE YELLOW WALLPAPER

AND OTHER STORIES OF LIBERATION

CHARLOTTE PERKINS GILMAN

Edited and Introduced by ULRICH BAER

CONTENTS

INTRODUCTION
Ulrich Baer

"Ain't I a woman?" Sojourner Truth's now-famous question, was not only rhetorical. Posed by the African American political activist at the 1851 Women's Convention in Akron, Ohio, to demand inclusion of African American women in the fight for the vote shortly after the Seneca Falls Convention of 1848, the question, which Truth answers in the affirmative, is in itself also a political statement. What it means to be a woman in the political context is not obvious, partly because politics was for so long defined by various exclusions of women. Thus the inquiry requires a broader rethinking of the political. Truth's deceptively simple question asks how the claim for one's identity rises to the level of political act rather than remaining little more than a personal, if empowering, assertion. How can the personal become political, that is to say, how can the insistence on one's private identity become the basis of political participation, which means the negotiation of individual and often conflicting (self-)interests for the sake of shared, communal existence? How can a woman's voice become a vehicle for change in a society that systematically excluded women from political life and, as part of this exclusion but also in the name of some universal concepts, treated every claim of personal identity as a challenge to the status quo? How does speaking as a woman transform politics?

Truth's "Ain't I a woman" challenged the burgeoning American women's movement to include African American women. That movement begins in the 1830s and reaches a first and important inflection point in 1920, when the 19th Amendment to the United

States Constitution grants women the right to vote, and then again in 1965, when the Voting Rights Act prohibits racial discrimination in voting and thus also grants African American women the right that Truth demanded over a century before. But Truth's question about asserting one's private identity as a source of authority is not settled with these political and legislative victories. The question of personal identity continues to challenge our understanding of which statements and actions count as political, and which statements and assertions of one's identity may be empowering but do not have to do with politics, that is the linking of an individual's concerns to those of others with very different and often contradictory concerns. Today, one hundred and seventy years after Truth's question first rang out as a clarion call for all political organizations yet to come into being, we still have not settled the debate of how to reconcile claims of subjective identity with political aims.

Saying "I am a woman" claims a space. But is this space political, or is it ultimately an utterance divorced from any political demand? If there is no successful step from private to political identity and the required sublimation of individuality for a greater cause, do individuals who insist on their identities produce competing claims for recognition, authority, and legitimacy, rather than transposing these competing claims into political action, here understood as jointly arranging our lives together? Claiming one's private identity can be enormously empowering. But can such a gesture, by itself, serve as the basis of political action, or does it atomize politics into as many competing individual claims as there are private identities?

What does this have to do with literature, and with women's writing in particular? The present volume gathers a set of key stories, all written by American women authors between the 1850s and 1930s—a period of unprecedented social and political change for women in the United States. These stories examine a wide range of issues that are often directly and dramatically, but not always exclusively, the result of the social ordering of individuals into strict categories of man or woman. These stories open up the question of gender, here understood as the social and political classification of individuals rather than an immutable biological truth, in various ways. In addition to being powerfully crafted and by now also critically acclaimed works with an influence far beyond the reach of their original publication, these stories show that defining the realm of politics as the necessary sublimation of personal identity for an overarching political program often means, ironically, propping up the patriarchy, where the voices and experiences of women and other historically marginalized groups are designed to matter less than those of men. Imaginative literature, here represented via the genre of the short story which flourished during this time in American publishing, offers readers access to a wider range of human experiences than those codified in politics and law. Far more than creating make-believe fantasy of no consequence, literary fiction offers ways of claiming identity that are not reducible to static assertions of a particular group's concerns—ways of reinventing both the individual and the group, both the private and the political. By creating new stories and a new language in which to account for our condition, writing by and about women has challenged the stark and unproductive division between private identity and political existence and shown how gender becomes a set of behaviors that is taught rather than a natural condition. But this also means that the category of "women's literature" cannot be reduced to literature written by women, or that the author's gender is the ultimate factor in determining a work's concerns or meaning. Literature in general—here meaning imaginative fiction, poetry, and plays—cannot be neatly mapped onto the social and political realms. In fact, imaginative literature explores and even invents new ways of claiming identity rather than merely affirming existing political categories. Speaking in one's own voice about one's own interests, especially in a culture that expects women to be silent, is a critical part of understanding oneself in relation to others.

Speaking in one's voice of things that are silenced in dominant culture, whether by fiat or due to the nature of experience, can be one
definition of literature. If statements about one's identity do not yet
qualify as properly political, they nonetheless open up a space from
which to think about how politics ought to function.

For these reasons, literary texts play a particular role in the many
efforts of allowing gender to be an enabling rather restrictive category.[1] They do not firmly establish an author's identity but provide
new lenses and frames through which to understand the categories of social vs. political identity. How do we transpose personal
identity into the political space of shared concerns and collective
action? How do we acknowledge the many differences between
people in a politics staked on equality? What is the role of language
in articulating our identities? Women's writing can offer a blueprint
for imagining the relation between social and political identity
beyond the apparent impasse of identity politics. Imaginative literature makes claims for the human condition from a particularized
vantage point, which may or may not coincide with the writer's
social and political identity. Because literature ascribes general
importance to personal identity without sacrificing its specificity,
the works of poetry and imaginative fiction bypass the dilemmas
posed by identity for politics. Women's literature, when understood
in this way, challenges false claims for universality in the guise of
intrinsic, artistic worth. But it also resists the simplistic equation of
a writer's social identity as a woman with the role of the author, and
the equally problematic equation of literature as yet another social
category in the political realm. The literary fiction in this anthology
imagines new ways of what it means to be a woman, and a man,
rather than simply transposing the author's social identity into the

1   For definitions of "gender" as a category of critical analysis, see Joan W.
Scott, "Gender: A Useful Category of Historical Analysis," in: *The American
Historical Review*, vol. 91, No. 5 (Dec., 1986, 1053-1075); Sandra Gilbert,
"Introduction," in: Sandra M. Gilbert and Susan Gubar, eds., *Feminist Literary
Theory and Criticism: A Norton Reader* (New York: Norton, 2007), 1-12.

literary realm. These short texts open up new identities rather than simply mirroring the social categories already found in politics. By claiming the right to free expression via literary texts, these authors imagine what political subjectivity and freedom mean on their own terms, rather than in the formulations provided by the reigning social order.

Today the term "identity politics" captures our unease about how best to link personal identity and political work. Politics, as earlier defined as the project of linking and embedding individual and often contradictory concerns anchored in very different life experiences in larger, shared projects—via solidarity, common interests, compromise, alliances, and other means of sublimating the individual into the collective—requires the shedding of personal identity for the sake of political identity. Instead of operating as individuals defending their interests defined by gender, ethnicity, religion, sexuality, or class, the political subject operates to achieve something with others who are and are not similar to themselves. If people insist too much on their subjective, private, or social identity, the arguments go, this self-assertion can block rather than aid in the political work of shaping our communal lives. Of course everyone needs to claim their identity in order to be recognized as a political subject, but if this assertion of identity is an end in itself, it renders politics impossible.

Women's writing, and women's imaginative fiction in particular, may chart a way out of the apparent tension between private identity and political participation. In a society where women's voices, experiences, bodies, and lives counted less than those of men or were entirely suppressed, women's assertions of their identity, especially when made in fiction, challenged the politics of their day. When women—the writers gathered in this anthology, for instance—use language to imagine and not only describe reality, they insist on being seen and recognized as fully enfranchised members of society. This part of being seen and recognized as authors is vitally important, to be sure; it remains part of the social and political program of affording all members of society opportunities of participation.

Women writers, and authors of fiction in particular, reimagine rather than take for granted what it means to speak as a woman, what it means to be a woman, and how the political and social categories of gender, including that of "woman writers," can and must be reconfigured to accommodate all. By using fiction to create believable characters beyond available stereotypes, writers expand the political category of gendered identity in powerful ways. Language, as novelist Toni Morrison explains in her 1993 Nobel Lecture, can be used to silence and strip vibrancy from life.[2] In fact, Truth's question, "Ain't I a woman," counters exactly that kind of language often used in politics and law, which denied her not only the right to vote but even enabled parts of the women's movement to refuse her claims of personhood as an African American woman. For this reason, I consider Truth's question to operate on the level of poetry in that it invests language with life rather than using language to silence and destroy.[3] The writers gathered in this volume

---

2   Toni Morrison, "Nobel Lecture," December 7, 1993, https://www. nobelprize.org/prizes/literature/1993/morrison/lecture/
3   In her "Nobel Lecture," Morrison identifies literature, or "unmolested language," as investing language "with life" rather than speaking in the name of silence. Morrison writes: "The old woman [in a parable] is keenly aware that no intellectual mercenary, nor insatiable dictator, no paid-for politician or demagogue; no counterfeit journalist would be persuaded by her thoughts. There is and will be rousing language to keep citizens armed and arming; slaughtered and slaughtering in the malls, courthouses, post offices, playgrounds, bedrooms and boulevards; stirring, memorializing language to mask the pity and waste of needless death. There will be more diplomatic language to countenance rape, torture, assassination. There is and will be more seductive, mutant language designed to throttle women, to pack their throats like paté-producing geese with their own unsayable, transgressive words; there will be more of the language of surveillance disguised as research; of politics and history calculated to render the suffering of millions mute; language glamorized to thrill the dissatisfied and bereft into assaulting their neighbors; arrogant pseudo-empirical language crafted to lock creative people into cages

use language in a similar way. They use language to activate our human potential to imagine ourselves and our lives differently, and through this act of the imagination to affect lasting change.

This collection of stories written by American women between 1859 and 1930—roughly covering the decades when women enter public life in unprecedented numbers in the United States—opens up additional ways of thinking of the relation between private identity and public life, during a period when women were relegated to secondary roles, or restricted or barred from participating in public activities. Several of these texts have become canonical, and all of the authors are today recognized for making significant contributions to the American canon. They do not eschew politics, and several of them, especially Frances Ellen Watkins Harper and Charlotte Perkins Gilman, were political activists who participated in public debates that shaped policies and political movements. But beyond and apart from exercising political influence, the stories gathered in this volume do something that is distinct from intervening in politics the way political speeches or manifestos can, as did texts by Susan B. Anthony, Elizabeth Cady Stanton, Anna Julia Cooper, Sojourner Truth, Frances Ellen Watkins Harper, and countless others who fought the political battle for freedom. Instead, these literary texts expand the horizon of what we imagine to be possible for women and for men, even if such newly imagined options were not yet part of the political vocabulary of the day.

As works of fiction, they do not cement but invent and broaden new categories of identity, including that of being a woman. By imagining new ways of existence, they also show how the traditional

---

of inferiority and hopelessness." By contrast, "[t]he vitality of language lies in its ability to limn the actual, imagined and possible lives of its speakers, readers, writers. Although its poise is sometimes in displacing experience it is not a substitute for it. It arcs toward the place where meaning may lie…Be it grand or slender, burrowing, blasting, or refusing to sanctify; whether it laughs out loud or is a cry without an alphabet, the choice word, the chosen silence, unmolested language surges toward knowledge, not its destruction."

conflict between politics and private identity may not be a prob-
lem inherent to modern democracy that must be resolved at the
expense of identity. Perhaps this conflict requires a rethinking of
politics altogether. And that work of reimagining depends on the
creative use of language found in stories such as these.

Differently put, political change is brought about not only
through politics but also, and importantly, through culture. Even
more to the point, it can be said that politics is "downstream" from
culture, meaning that real change starts with and requires the proverbial change of minds and hearts which politics and law cast into
institutional and legal forms. This means, in the case of literature,
describing not only the reality that we consider possible but also
reaching toward the ineffable, the seemingly unimaginable, the forbidden, the silenced, and the utopian. Several stories in this anthology propose something different from the dominant idea that in
order to be a political subject, we must disguise, suppress, or shed
our private identity. They show how this conception of politics often
means that women in particular have to deny, lose, or obscure part
of their identity to become genuine rather than gendered political
subjects, while male-identified individuals happen to appear like
neutral, universal beings. It is not only the definition of individual
existence that fails to account for women's experience, but also the
definition of politics.

Rather than critiquing the prevailing idea of politics as universal and collective or presenting women's experiences as inevitably
acts of resistance, women's imaginative literature charts a different
course. Like all literature of significance, the stories in this anthology present fictional characters and situations that are rendered
with sufficient authenticity, i.e., internal coherence, to reflect and
also alter our experience of being in the world. Gender is important
but it is not the only category in these texts, here understood as the
experience of difference and sexuality, and the political and social
status assigned to women and men according to biological gender.

The heroines in these stories rebel and conform, resist and accommodate, speak up and remain silent. They do not follow a single path but explore what it means to be a woman starting in mid-nineteenth-century America, when great numbers of women became part of public life in previously unknown ways. In many ways, the mere fact that these stories center on women who are more than stereotypes already defies most mainstream literary conventions of the period. There are important exceptions to the mainstream reductive image of women or to the simple absence of fully developed women characters outside of the conventional romantic plot. The point of this anthology is to show the breadth of fiction written by women about women from various perspectives.

In her short 1913 note on "Why I Wrote the Yellow Wallpaper," published about two decades after the story first appeared in 1892, Charlotte Perkins Gilman records her doctor's 1887 recommendation "never to touch pen, brush or pencil again as long as I lived." She had supposedly "suffered from a severe and continuous nervous breakdown tending to melancholia—and beyond," and was advised to "live as domestic a life as far as possible." After initially obeying those directions, she "cast the noted specialist's advice"—rooted in the larger belief that women should remain silent "angels in the house" with no public roles and no public statements—"to the winds and went to work again." She published a text today considered a key work in the feminist canon, which comprises all of the works that do not accept facile and ultimately inauthentic representations of what it means to be a woman and a man under the conditions of the patriarchy.[4] Gilman's text, as well as the other stories in this collection, describe but also *invent* what it means to be a woman, rather than condone or revolt against existing definitions of gender. This does not mean that these stories are merely speculative flights

---

4   One of the central interpretations of Gilman's text is Paula A. Treichler, "Escaping the Sentence: Diagnosis and Discourse in 'The Yellow Wallpaper,'" in: *Tulsa Studies in Women's Literature,* vol. 3, no.1/2 Vol. 3, No. 1/2 (Spring–Autumn, 1984), 61-77.

of fancy, whereas political speeches make concrete interventions in reality. It means that they use gender as both a social and political category and an open-ended idea that can be continually reimagined and redefined.

For many readers, "The Yellow Wallpaper" has become shorthand for a woman's protest against the control, manipulation, and confinement experienced by many women at the hands of men who claim to care for them.[5] Gilman's text, like much of (though by no means all) women's writing, harnesses the power of imaginative fiction to challenge and change mainstream culture, which privileges the experience and voices of men at the expense of women. It has prompted a great number of critical responses and is often cited as a central text in the explosion of women's writing starting in the late nineteenth century, when social, economic, and political conditions change sufficiently to allow women to find the actual and metaphoric "room of one's own" necessary for creative work, as stated in Frances Ellen Watkins Harper's 1872 poem about a formerly enslaved women intent on reading as a path to self-determination against a succession of opposing forces of enslavers, political leaders, and even her own family, and later in Virginia Woolf's memorable phrase in her 1929 essay on the conditions for women's literature through the ages.[6] But its paradigmatic status should not lead us to think that women's literature is invariably a literature of

---

5   Susan Lanser has argued that "The Yellow Wallpaper" assumed its key role as a foundational text in American feminist studies because it consolidates a white American identity rather than achieves a genuine reflection on difference. Her insightful essay explains how Gilman's story became an ur-text of feminist criticism at the expense of a more inclusive conception of feminism, and how to reconcile Gilman's conservative or reactionary views on the diversity of American life in her time with her progressive politics. See Susan S. Lanser, "Feminist Criticism, 'The Yellow Wallpaper,' and the Politics of Color in America," Feminist Studies, 15: 3 (Autumn, 1989), 415-441.
6   Frances Ellen Watkins Harper, "Learning to Read," reprinted in Ulrich Baer and Smaran Dayal, eds., *Fictions of America: The Book of Firsts* (New York: Warbler Press 2021), 186; Virginia Woolf, *A Room of One's Own*, introduction by Susan Gubar (New York: Mariner Books, 2005).

protest against male domination. "The Yellow Wallpaper" is one of a great network of women's literature where use of voice, meaning the speaker's intent, is linked to quality of voice, meaning how the speaker is heard by others. These countless stories, novels, plays, and poems written by women about their experiences on their own terms challenge the idea that the literary canon as it has been transmitted reflects human experience in its totality, and that the categories by which literary texts have been evaluated are neutral and objective, without a bias in favor of male-authored texts. A great canon of writers, scholars, activists, and critics, including Virginia Woolf, Simone de Beauvoir, Kate Millet, Doris Lessing, Sandra Gilbert, Susan Gubar, Julia Kristeva, Hélène Cixous, Hortense Spillers, Frances Smith Foster, Toril Moi, Audre Lorde, Elaine Showalter, Hazel Carby, bell hooks, Carol Gilligan, Catharine Stimpson, Shoshana Felman, and many others used a feminist lens to explain how social conceptions of gender cannot be mapped onto literary texts without distortion, and how literature explores new ways of conceptualizing gender rather than replicating social categories.[7]

Many of these stories have contributed to the seismic transformation of the human condition ushered in by the full participation of women in both private and public life. Today, we tend to think of women's movements as modern political forces that formed after the creation of nation states in the late eighteenth century, when non-elites fought for formal participation in politics. Since women were systematically excluded from the sphere of politics, their activism by default involved the sphere of culture, where definitions are revised, negotiated, and invented rather than serve to stabilize

---

7   On feminist interpretations of literature, see: *The Cambridge Companion to Feminist Literary Theory,* ed. Ellen Rooney (Cambridge: Cambridge University Press, 2006); *Feminist Literary Theory and Criticism: A Norton Reader,* eds. Sandra M Gilbert and Susan Gubar (New York: W.W. Norton, 2007); *Critical Terms for the Study of Gender,* eds. Catharine R. Stimpson and Gilbert Herdt (Chicago: University of Chicago, 2014).

identity. Long before women organized politically in ways familiar to us today, women spoke about their experiences and challenged the pernicious idea that the difference between the sexes implies an innate hierarchy and men's inherent superiority. A significant record of this speech is women's literature. Literature is consequently a key aspect of this transformation of the human condition, because through it people expressed themselves—the restrictions on publishing notwithstanding—when public discourse and the definitions of appropriate gender roles excluded them. In the case of women's writing, it means that authors had to invent new ways and new voices to depict the human experience; as feminist critics have noted, this does not mean that women's writing is limited to texts written by women.

We present Gilman's key story, "The Yellow Wallpaper," in the context of nine other equally powerful stories by female American authors. All of these stories are concerned on the level of plot with women's existence in modern society. But like all great literature, each of these stories also changes familiar techniques of storytelling to present the situation of women whose experience and means of expressing it are shaped by forces not their own. These stories invite us to consider whether a woman's way of knowing about and being in the world is a distinct mode of existence and whether this existence can become the center from which to account for one's life on its own terms rather than as something "different" from the mainstream (that is, putatively neutral but in reality masculine) point of view.

All great literature claims a unique position from which to regard and experience the world slightly askance from dominant and therefore standardized, routinized ways of seeing. Women's literature claims such a unique perspective, as expressed in Zora Neale Hurston's story "Sweat": "Nobody but a woman could tell how she knew this even before she struck the match." Given the stubborn ways of socializing human beings into gendered individuals, we still have no good way of accounting for this unique perspective occupied by women without labeling it as "different." "Different from what?" all of these stories ask. Different from whose definition of what counts as "normal," "traditional," "acceptable," "sane," "healthy," "mainstream," "proper," and "appropriate"? Different from the way men have tried not only to shape women's lives but also tell women how to experience and speak about those lives, and how men have told women not to speak and say what men considered unspeakable, inappropriate, and scandalous? Different from the recommendations and actions by fathers, brothers, husbands, teachers, priests, and doctors to lock women up, sedate, control, lobotomize, and otherwise restrain them, which is the literal rather than metaphoric point of Gilman's story?

But perhaps women's writing undoes the obdurate idea that there exists a proper way of talking of one's experience, and then there exists "difference" which deviates from the norm. When seen through a woman's eyes, the world looks different from the world that is centered on male experience. Perhaps it is different even from the idea that the self constitutes the center of experience.

But what this reveals is not difference itself, or the existence and importance of gender, but the fact that the male perspective is not neutral and self-identical but has been imposed on everyone—female, male, or non-binary—by human action rather than divine will or natural laws. Instead of considering these stories to be critical deviations from a canon of great texts that registers women's voices as marking a difference, we present this collection of stories by American women writers from vastly different backgrounds, artistic interests, and literary styles, as the multipronged beginnings of a new tradition.

Frances Ellen Watkins Harper's story "The Two Offers" (1859), which also happens to be the first known story published by an African American woman in the United States, explores whether a women's choice to marry either for the "over-mastering passion" of love or for material stability is flawed, "because no perfect womanhood is developed by imperfect culture." Harper's tale ends with the adage "that true happiness consists [...] in the regulation of desires and the full development and right culture of our whole natures," but leaves open what a "right culture" could mean where both women and men can live authentically. Elizabeth Stoddard's 1864 story "The Prescription," about a doctor ordering a woman to temporarily separate from her husband, foreshadows the basic points of Gilman's tale, but charts a different notion of personal liberty and narrative redemption. Kate Chopin's paradigmatic 1894 "Story of an Hour" describes a woman's life choices in the span of an afternoon punctured with two instances of disturbing news with such cutting irony that even today the ending may startle a reader's conception of propriety. Edith Wharton's 1902 "The Reckoning" examines how personal freedom may be reconciled with the idea of marriage when both partners have equal choices rather than choices defined by gender stereotypes. Sui Sin Far's 1910 "Mrs. Spring Fragrance," by the first Asian American writer known to publish fiction in the United States, subtly undermines conventional ideas of feminine empathy by recounting a Chinese American woman's intervention in a neighbor's love life against the backdrop of cultural differences between first-generation immigrants and their American-born children. Gertrude Stein's "Miss Furr and Miss Skeene," originally written in 1910 or 1911 and published in 1922, by one of the paragons of experimental modernist fiction, is a literary romp of great wit and verve that tells of two women very gaily in love. Djuna Barnes's 1916 story "What Do You See, Madam?" explores how women can present themselves to a public which craves stereotypes in the context of a vaudeville show, and how a woman may use such stereotypes to express a countercultural truth. Zora Neale Hurston's 1926 story "Sweat" is about an African American woman who makes a morally ambiguous choice when her abusive husband suffers his horrific comeuppance in the fangs of a rattlesnake. Hurston's depiction of strong female characters—also found in her American masterpiece, the 1937 novel *Their Eyes Were Watching God*—offers yet another perspective of what it means to be and to write as a woman. The anthology's final entry is Nella Larsen's 1930 story "Sanctuary," where a mother is forced into an impossible choice between the racist and patriarchal law enforcement in her community and the love for her murdered son.

All of the texts in this anthology challenge the ideas that a woman's identity is defined exclusively by the society in which she lives, and that the assertion of personal identity is an obstacle to the work of politics, where private identity must surrender to larger concerns. They posit gender and women not as the difference to an unspoken norm but as another way of centering human experience as the nexus of the private and the public.

Two decades into the twenty-first century, it seems evident that the question of gender remains an unresolved issue around the world, even if the patriarchy's pernicious impact on all human beings has been challenged. How children are socialized into becoming boys and girls, and how courageous individuals challenge and live out new notions of gender that do not trap people into unworkable sets of behavior and expectations is of vital importance. Since these efforts are not only the business of politics but also always feats of the imagination, the stories in this collection continue to inspire and energize such efforts even today.

THE YELLOW WALLPAPER[1]

Charlotte Perkins Gilman

IT IS VERY seldom that mere ordinary people like John and myself secure ancestral halls for the summer.

A colonial mansion, a hereditary estate, I would say a haunted house, and reach the height of romantic felicity—but that would be asking too much of fate!

Still I will proudly declare that there is something queer about it.

Else, why should it be let so cheaply? And why have stood so long untenanted?

John laughs at me, of course, but one expects that in marriage.

John is practical in the extreme. He has no patience with faith, an intense horror of superstition, and he scoffs openly at any talk of things not to be felt and seen and put down in figures.

John is a physician, and *perhaps*—(I would not say it to a living soul, of course, but this is dead paper and a great relief to my mind)—*perhaps* that is one reason I do not get well faster.

You see, he does not believe I am sick!

And what can one do?

If a physician of high standing, and one's own husband, assures friends and relatives that there is really nothing the matter with one but temporary nervous depression—a slight hysterical tendency—what is one to do?

My brother is also a physician, and also of high standing, and he says the same thing.

So I take phosphates or phosphites—whichever it is, and tonics,

---

1   First published in *The New England Magazine,* January 1892.

and journeys, and air, and exercise, and am absolutely forbidden to "work" until I am well again.

Personally, I disagree with their ideas.

Personally, I believe that congenial work, with excitement and change, would do me good.

But what is one to do?

I did write for a while in spite of them; but it *does* exhaust me a good deal—having to be so sly about it, or else meet with heavy opposition.

I sometimes fancy that in my condition if I had less opposition and more society and stimulus—but John says the very worst thing I can do is to think about my condition, and I confess it always makes me feel bad.

So I will let it alone and talk about the house.

The most beautiful place! It is quite alone, standing well back from the road, quite three miles from the village. It makes me think of English places that you read about, for there are hedges and walls and gates that lock, and lots of separate little houses for the gardeners and people.

There is a *delicious* garden! I never saw such a garden—large and shady, full of box-bordered paths, and lined with long grape-covered arbors with seats under them.

There were greenhouses, too, but they are all broken now.

There was some legal trouble, I believe, something about the heirs and co-heirs; anyhow, the place has been empty for years.

That spoils my ghostliness, I am afraid; but I don't care—there is something strange about the house—I can feel it.

I even said so to John one moonlight evening, but he said what I felt was a *draught*, and shut the window.

I get unreasonably angry with John sometimes. I'm sure I never used to be so sensitive. I think it is due to this nervous condition.

But John says if I feel so I shall neglect proper self-control; so I take pains to control myself,—before him, at least,—and that makes me very tired.

I don't like our room a bit. I wanted one downstairs that opened on the piazza and had roses all over the window, and such pretty old-fashioned chintz hangings! but John would not hear of it.

He said there was only one window and not room for two beds, and no near room for him if he took another.

He is very careful and loving, and hardly lets me stir without special direction.

I have a schedule prescription for each hour in the day; he takes all care from me, and so I feel basely ungrateful not to value it more.

He said we came here solely on my account, that I was to have perfect rest and all the air I could get. "Your exercise depends on your strength, my dear," said he, "and your food somewhat on your appetite; but air you can absorb all the time." So we took the nursery, at the top of the house.

It is a big, airy room, the whole floor nearly, with windows that look all ways, and air and sunshine galore. It was nursery first and then playground and gymnasium, I should judge; for the windows are barred for little children, and there are rings and things in the walls.

The paint and paper look as if a boys' school had used it. It is stripped off—the paper—in great patches all around the head of my bed, about as far as I can reach, and in a great place on the other side of the room low down. I never saw a worse paper in my life.

One of those sprawling flamboyant patterns committing every artistic sin.

It is dull enough to confuse the eye in following, pronounced enough to constantly irritate, and provoke study, and when you follow the lame, uncertain curves for a little distance they suddenly commit suicide—plunge off at outrageous angles, destroy themselves in unheard-of contradictions.

The color is repellant, almost revolting; a smouldering, unclean yellow, strangely faded by the slow-turning sunlight.

It is a dull yet lurid orange in some places, a sickly sulphur tint in others.

No wonder the children hated it! I should hate it myself if I had to live in this room long.

There comes John, and I must put this away,—he hates to have me write a word.

We have been here two weeks, and I haven't felt like writing before, since that first day.

I am sitting by the window now, up in this atrocious nursery, and there is nothing to hinder my writing as much as I please, save lack of strength.

John is away all day, and even some nights when his cases are serious.

I am glad my case is not serious!

But these nervous troubles are dreadfully depressing.

John does not know how much I really suffer. He knows there is no *reason* to suffer, and that satisfies him.

Of course it is only nervousness. It does weigh on me so not to do my duty in any way!

I meant to be such a help to John, such a real rest and comfort, and here I am a comparative burden already!

Nobody would believe what an effort it is to do what little I am able—to dress and entertain, and order things.

It is fortunate Mary is so good with the baby. Such a dear baby!

And yet I *cannot* be with him, it makes me so nervous.

I suppose John never was nervous in his life. He laughs at me so about this wallpaper!

At first he meant to repaper the room, but afterwards he said that I was letting it get the better of me, and that nothing was worse for a nervous patient than to give way to such fancies.

He said that after the wallpaper was changed it would be the heavy bedstead, and then the barred windows, and then that gate at the head of the stairs, and so on.

"You know the place is doing you good," he said, "and really, dear, I don't care to renovate the house just for a three months' rental."

"Then do let us go downstairs," I said, "there are such pretty rooms there."

Then he took me in his arms and called me a blessed little goose, and said he would go down cellar if I wished, and have it whitewashed into the bargain.

But he is right enough about the beds and windows and things.

It is as airy and comfortable a room as any one need wish, and, of course, I would not be so silly as to make him uncomfortable just for a whim.

I'm really getting quite fond of the big room, all but that horrid paper.

Out of one window I can see the garden, those mysterious deep-shaded arbors, the riotous old-fashioned flowers, and bushes and gnarly trees.

Out of another I get a lovely view of the bay and a little private wharf belonging to the estate. There is a beautiful shaded lane that runs down there from the house. I always fancy I see people walking in these numerous paths and arbors, but John has cautioned me not to give way to fancy in the least. He says that with my imaginative power and habit of story-making a nervous weakness like mine is sure to lead to all manner of excited fancies, and that I ought to use my will and good sense to check the tendency. So I try.

I think sometimes that if I were only well enough to write a little it would relieve the press of ideas and rest me.

But I find I get pretty tired when I try.

It is so discouraging not to have any advice and companionship about my work. When I get really well John says we will ask Cousin Henry and Julia down for a long visit; but he says he would as soon put fire-works in my pillow-case as to let me have those stimulating people about now.

I wish I could get well faster.

But I must not think about that. This paper looks to me as if it *knew* what a vicious influence it had!

There is a recurrent spot where the pattern lolls like a broken neck and two bulbous eyes stare at you upside-down.

I get positively angry with the impertinence of it and the everlastingness. Up and down and sideways they crawl, and those absurd, unblinking eyes are everywhere. There is one place where two breadths didn't match, and the eyes go all up and down the line, one a little higher than the other.

I never saw so much expression in an inanimate thing before, and we all know how much expression they have! I used to lie awake as a child and get more entertainment and terror out of blank walls and plain furniture than most children could find in a toy-store.

I remember what a kindly wink the knobs of our big old bureau used to have, and there was one chair that always seemed like a strong friend.

I used to feel that if any of the other things looked too fierce I could always hop into that chair and be safe.

The furniture in this room is no worse than inharmonious, however, for we had to bring it all from downstairs. I suppose when this was used as a playroom they had to take the nursery things out, and no wonder! I never saw such ravages as the children have made here.

The wallpaper, as I said before, is torn off in spots, and it sticketh closer than a brother—they must have had perseverance as well as hatred.

Then the floor is scratched and gouged and splintered, the plaster itself is dug out here and there, and this great heavy bed, which is all we found in the room, looks as if it had been through the wars.

But I don't mind it a bit—only the paper.

There comes John's sister. Such a dear girl as she is, and so careful of me! I must not let her find me writing.

She is a perfect, and enthusiastic housekeeper, and hopes for no better profession. I verily believe she thinks it is the writing which made me sick!

But I can write when she is out, and see her a long way off from these windows.

There is one that commands the road, a lovely, shaded, winding road, and one that just looks off over the country. A lovely country, too, full of great elms and velvet meadows.

This wallpaper has a kind of sub-pattern in a different shade, a particularly irritating one, for you can only see it in certain lights, and not clearly then.

But in the places where it isn't faded, and where the sun is just so, I can see a strange, provoking, formless sort of figure, that seems to sulk about behind that silly and conspicuous front design.

There's sister on the stairs!

Well, the Fourth of July is over! The people are gone and I am tired out. John thought it might do me good to see a little company, so we just had mother and Nellie and the children down for a week.

Of course I didn't do a thing. Jennie sees to everything now.

But it tired me all the same.

John says if I don't pick up faster he shall send me to Weir Mitchell in the fall.

But I don't want to go there at all. I had a friend who was in his hands once, and she says he is just like John and my brother, only more so!

Besides, it is such an undertaking to go so far.

I don't feel as if it was worth while to turn my hand over for anything, and I'm getting dreadfully fretful and querulous.

I cry at nothing, and cry most of the time.

Of course I don't when John is here, or anybody else, but when I am alone.

And I am alone a good deal just now. John is kept in town very often by serious cases, and Jennie is good and lets me alone when I want her to.

So I walk a little in the garden or down that lovely lane, sit on the porch under the roses, and lie down up here a good deal.

I'm getting really fond of the room in spite of the wallpaper. Perhaps *because* of the wallpaper.

It dwells in my mind so!

I lie here on this great immovable bed—it is nailed down, I believe—and follow that pattern about by the hour. It is as good as gymnastics, I assure you. I start, we'll say, at the bottom, down in the corner over there where it has not been touched, and I determine for the thousandth time that I *will* follow that pointless pattern to some sort of a conclusion.

I know a little of the principle of design, and I know this thing was not arranged on any laws of radiation, or alternation, or repetition, or symmetry, or anything else that I ever heard of.

It is repeated, of course, by the breadths, but not otherwise.

Looked at in one way each breadth stands alone, the bloated curves and flourishes—a kind of "debased Romanesque" with *delirium tremens*—go waddling up and down in isolated columns of fatuity.

But, on the other hand, they connect diagonally, and the sprawling outlines run off in great slanting waves of optic horror, like a lot of wallowing seaweeds in full chase.

The whole thing goes horizontally, too, at least it seems so, and I exhaust myself in trying to distinguish the order of its going in that direction.

They have used a horizontal breadth for a frieze, and that adds wonderfully to the confusion.

There is one end of the room where it is almost intact, and there, when the cross-lights fade and the low sun shines directly upon it, I can almost fancy radiation after all,—the interminable grotesques seem to form around a common centre and rush off in headlong plunges of equal distraction.

It makes me tired to follow it. I will take a nap, I guess.

I don't know why I should write this.

I don't want to.

I don't feel able.

And I know John would think it absurd. But I *must* say what I feel and think in some way—it is such a relief!

But the effort is getting to be greater than the relief.

Half the time now I am awfully lazy, and lie down ever so much.

John says I musn't lose my strength, and has me take cod-liver oil and lots of tonics and things, to say nothing of ale and wine and rare meat.

Dear John! He loves me very dearly, and hates to have me sick. I tried to have a real earnest reasonable talk with him the other day, and tell him how I wish he would let me go and make a visit to Cousin Henry and Julia.

But he said I wasn't able to go, nor able to stand it after I got there; and I did not make out a very good case for myself, for I was crying before I had finished.

It is getting to be a great effort for me to think straight. Just this nervous weakness, I suppose.

And dear John gathered me up in his arms, and just carried me upstairs and laid me on the bed, and sat by me and read to me till it tired my head.

He said I was his darling and his comfort and all he had, and that I must take care of myself for his sake, and keep well.

He says no one but myself can help me out of it, that I must use my will and self-control and not let any silly fancies run away with me.

There's one comfort, the baby is well and happy, and does not have to occupy this nursery with the horrid wallpaper.

If we had not used it that blessed child would have! What a fortunate escape! Why, I wouldn't have a child of mine, an impressionable little thing, live in such a room for worlds.

I never thought of it before, but it is lucky that John kept me here after all. I can stand it so much easier than a baby, you see.

Of course I never mention it to them any more,—I am too wise,—but I keep watch of it all the same.

There are things in that paper that nobody knows but me, or ever will.

Behind that outside pattern the dim shapes get clearer every day.

It is always the same shape, only very numerous.

And it is like a woman stooping down and creeping about behind that pattern. I don't like it a bit. I wonder—I begin to think—I wish John would take me away from here!

It is so hard to talk with John about my case, because he is so wise, and because he loves me so.

But I tried it last night.

It was moonlight. The moon shines in all around, just as the sun does.

I hate to see it sometimes, it creeps so slowly, and always comes in by one window or another.

John was asleep and I hated to waken him, so I kept still and watched the moonlight on that undulating wallpaper till I felt creepy.

The faint figure behind seemed to shake the pattern, just as if she wanted to get out.

I got up softly and went to feel and see if the paper *did* move, and when I came back John was awake.

"What is it, little girl?" he said. "Don't go walking about like that—you'll get cold."

I thought it was a good time to talk, so I told him that I really was not gaining here, and that I wished he would take me away.

"Why darling!" said he, "our lease will be up in three weeks, and I can't see how to leave before.

"The repairs are not done at home, and I cannot possibly leave town just now. Of course if you were in any danger I could and would, but you really are better, dear, whether you can see it or not.

I am a doctor, dear, and I know. You are gaining flesh and color, your appetite is better. I feel really much easier about you."

"I don't weigh a bit more," said I, "nor as much; and my appetite may be better in the evening, when you are here, but it is worse in the morning when you are away."

"Bless her little heart!" said he with a big hug; "she shall be as sick as she pleases! But now let's improve the shining hours by going to sleep, and talk about it in the morning!"

"And you won't go away?" I asked gloomily.

"Why, how can I, dear? It is only three weeks more and then we will take a nice little trip of a few days while Jennie is getting the house ready. Really, dear, you are better!"

"Better in body perhaps"—I began, and stopped short, for he sat up straight and looked at me with such a stern, reproachful look that I could not say another word.

"My darling," said he, "I beg of you, for my sake and for our child's sake, as well as for your own, that you will never for one instant let that idea enter your mind! There is nothing so dangerous, so fascinating, to a temperament like yours. It is a false and foolish fancy. Can you not trust me as a physician when I tell you so?"

So of course I said no more on that score, and we went to sleep before long. He thought I was asleep first, but I wasn't,—I lay there for hours trying to decide whether that front pattern and the back pattern really did move together or separately.

On a pattern like this, by daylight, there is a lack of sequence, a defiance of law, that is a constant irritant to a normal mind.

The color is hideous enough, and unreliable enough, and infuriating enough, but the pattern is torturing.

You think you have mastered it, but just as you get well under way in following, it turns a back somersault and there you are. It slaps you in the face, knocks you down, and tramples upon you. It is like a bad dream.

The outside pattern is a florid arabesque, reminding one of a fungus. If you can imagine a toadstool in joints, an interminable string of toadstools, budding and sprouting in endless convolutions,—why, that is something like it.

That is, sometimes!

There is one marked peculiarity about this paper, a thing nobody seems to notice but myself, and that is that it changes as the light changes.

When the sun shoots in through the east window—I always watch for that first long, straight ray—it changes so quickly that I never can quite believe it.

That is why I watch it always.

By moonlight—the moon shines in all night when there is a moon—I wouldn't know it was the same paper.

At night in any kind of light, in twilight, candlelight, lamplight, and worst of all by moonlight, it becomes bars! The outside pattern I mean, and the woman behind it is as plain as can be.

I didn't realize for a long time what the thing was that showed behind,—that dim sub-pattern,—but now I am quite sure it is a woman.

By daylight she is subdued, quiet. I fancy it is the pattern that keeps her so still. It is so puzzling. It keeps me quiet by the hour.

I lie down ever so much now. John says it is good for me, and to sleep all I can.

Indeed, he started the habit by making me lie down for an hour after each meal.

It is a very bad habit, I am convinced, for, you see, I don't sleep.

And that cultivates deceit, for I don't tell them I'm awake,—oh, no!

The fact is, I am getting a little afraid of John.

He seems very queer sometimes, and even Jennie has an inexplicable look.

It strikes me occasionally, just as a scientific hypothesis, that perhaps it is the paper!

I have watched John when he did not know I was looking, and come into the room suddenly on the most innocent excuses, and I've caught him several times *looking at the paper!* And Jennie too. I caught Jennie with her hand on it once.

She didn't know I was in the room, and when I asked her in a quiet, a very quiet voice, with the most restrained manner possible, what she was doing with the paper she turned around as if she had been caught stealing, and looked quite angry—asked me why I should frighten her so!

Then she said that the paper stained everything it touched, that she had found yellow smooches on all my clothes and John's, and she wished we would be more careful!

Did not that sound innocent? But I know she was studying that pattern, and I am determined that nobody shall find it out but myself!

Life is very much more exciting now than it used to be. You see I have something more to expect, to look forward to, to watch. I really do eat better, and am more quiet than I was.

John is so pleased to see me improve! He laughed a little the other day, and said I seemed to be flourishing in spite of my wallpaper.

I turned it off with a laugh. I had no intention of telling him it was *because* of the wallpaper—he would make fun of me. He might even want to take me away.

I don't want to leave now until I have found it out. There is a week more, and I think that will be enough.

I'm feeling ever so much better! I don't sleep much at night, for it is so interesting to watch developments; but I sleep a good deal in the daytime.

In the daytime it is tiresome and perplexing.

There are always new shoots on the fungus, and new shades of yellow all over it. I cannot keep count of them, though I have tried conscientiously.

It is the strangest yellow, that wallpaper! It makes me think of all the yellow things I ever saw—not beautiful ones like buttercups, but old foul, bad yellow things.

But there is something else about that paper—the smell! I noticed it the moment we came into the room, but with so much air and sun it was not bad. Now we have had a week of fog and rain, and whether the windows are open or not, the smell is here.

It creeps all over the house.

I find it hovering in the dining-room, skulking in the parlor, hiding in the hall, lying in wait for me on the stairs.

It gets into my hair.

Even when I go to ride, if I turn my head suddenly and surprise it—there is that smell!

Such a peculiar odor, too! I have spent hours in trying to analyze it, to find what it smelled like.

It is not bad—at first, and very gentle, but quite the subtlest, most enduring odor I ever met.

In this damp weather it is awful. I wake up in the night and find it hanging over me.

It used to disturb me at first. I thought seriously of burning the house—to reach the smell.

But now I am used to it. The only thing I can think of that it is like is the *color* of the paper! A yellow smell.

There is a very funny mark on this wall, low down, near the mopboard. A streak that runs round the room. It goes behind every piece of furniture, except the bed, a long, straight, even *smooch*, as if it had been rubbed over and over.

I wonder how it was done and who did it, and what they did it for. Round and round and round—round and round and round—it makes me dizzy!

I really have discovered something at last.

Through watching so much at night, when it changes so, I have finally found out.

The front pattern *does* move—and no wonder! The woman

behind shakes it!

Sometimes I think there are a great many women behind, and sometimes only one, and she crawls around fast, and her crawling shakes it all over.

Then in the very bright spots she keeps still, and in the very shady spots she just takes hold of the bars and shakes them hard.

And she is all the time trying to climb through. But nobody could climb through that pattern—it strangles so; I think that is why it has so many heads.

They get through, and then the pattern strangles them off and turns them upside-down, and makes their eyes white!

If those heads were covered or taken off it would not be half so bad.

I think that woman gets out in the daytime!

And I'll tell you why—privately—I've seen her!

I can see her out of every one of my windows!

It is the same woman, I know, for she is always creeping, and most women do not creep by daylight.

I see her on that long shaded lane, creeping up and down. I see her in those dark grape arbors, creeping all around the garden.

I see her on that long road under the trees, creeping along, and when a carriage comes she hides under the blackberry vines.

I don't blame her a bit. It must be very humiliating to be caught creeping by daylight!

I always lock the door when I creep by daylight. I can't do it at night, for I know John would suspect something at once.

And John is so queer now, that I don't want to irritate him. I wish he would take another room! Besides, I don't want anybody to get that woman out at night but myself.

I often wonder if I could see her out of all the windows at once.

But, turn as fast as I can, I can only see out of one at one time.

And though I always see her she *may* be able to creep faster than I can turn!

I have watched her sometimes away off in the open country, creeping as fast as a cloud shadow in a high wind.

If only that top pattern could be gotten off from the under one! I mean to try it, little by little.

I have found out another funny thing, but I shan't tell it this time! It does not do to trust people too much.

There are only two more days to get this paper off, and I believe John is beginning to notice. I don't like the look in his eyes.

And I heard him ask Jennie a lot of professional questions about me. She had a very good report to give.

She said I slept a good deal in the daytime.

John knows I don't sleep very well at night, for all I'm so quiet!

He asked me all sorts of questions, too, and pretended to be very loving and kind.

As if I couldn't see through him!

Still, I don't wonder he acts so, sleeping under this paper for three months.

It only interests me, but I feel sure John and Jennie are secretly affected by it.

Hurrah! This is the last day, but it is enough. John is to stay in town over night, and won't be out until this evening.

Jennie wanted to sleep with me—the sly thing! but I told her I should undoubtedly rest better for a night all alone.

That was clever, for really I wasn't alone a bit! As soon as it was moonlight, and that poor thing began to crawl and shake the pattern, I got up and ran to help her.

I pulled and she shook, I shook and she pulled, and before morning we had peeled off yards of that paper.

A strip about as high as my head and half around the room.

And then when the sun came and that awful pattern began to laugh at me I declared I would finish it to-day!

We go away to-morrow, and they are moving all my furniture down again to leave things as they were before.

Jennie looked at the wall in amazement, but I told her merrily that I did it out of pure spite at the vicious thing.

She laughed and said she wouldn't mind doing it herself, but I must not get tired.

How she betrayed herself that time!

But I am here, and no person touches this paper but me—not *alive!*

She tried to get me out of the room—it was too patent! But I said it was so quiet and empty and clean now that I believed I would lie down again and sleep all I could; and not to wake me even for dinner—I would call when I woke.

So now she is gone, and the servants are gone, and the things are gone, and there is nothing left but that great bedstead nailed down, with the canvas mattress we found on it.

We shall sleep downstairs to-night, and take the boat home to-morrow.

I quite enjoy the room, now it is bare again.

How those children did tear about here!

This bedstead is fairly gnawed!

But I must get to work.

I have locked the door and thrown the key down into the front path.

I don't want to go out, and I don't want to have anybody come in, till John comes.

I want to astonish him.

I've got a rope up here that even Jennie did not find. If that woman does get out, and tries to get away, I can tie her!

But I forgot I could not reach far without anything to stand on!

This bed will *not* move!

I tried to lift and push it until I was lame, and then I got so angry I bit off a little piece at one corner—but it hurt my teeth.

Then I peeled off all the paper I could reach standing on the floor. It sticks horribly and the pattern just enjoys it! All those strangled heads and bulbous eyes and waddling fungus growths just shriek with derision!

I am getting angry enough to do something desperate. To jump out of the window would be admirable exercise, but the bars are too strong even to try.

Besides I wouldn't do it. Of course not. I know well enough that a step like that is improper and might be misconstrued.

I don't like to *look* out of the windows even—there are so many of those creeping women, and they creep so fast.

I wonder if they all come out of that wallpaper as I did?

But I am securely fastened now by my well-hidden rope—you don't get *me* out in the road there!

I suppose I shall have to get back behind the pattern when it comes night, and that is hard!

It is so pleasant to be out in this great room and creep around as I please!

I don't want to go outside. I won't, even if Jennie asks me to.

For outside you have to creep on the ground, and everything is green instead of yellow.

But here I can creep smoothly on the floor, and my shoulder just fits in that long smooch around the wall, so I cannot lose my way.

Why, there's John at the door!

It is no use, young man, you can't open it!

How he does call and pound!

Now he's crying for an axe.

It would be a shame to break down that beautiful door!

"John dear!" said I in the gentlest voice, "the key is down by the front steps, under a plantain leaf!"

That silenced him for a few moments.

Then he said—very quietly indeed, "Open the door, my darling!"

"I can't," said I. "The key is down by the front door under a plantain leaf!"

And then I said it again, several times, very gently and slowly, and said it so often that he had to go and see, and he got it, of course, and came in. He stopped short by the door.

"What is the matter?" he cried. "For God's sake, what are you doing!"

I kept on creeping just the same, but I looked at him over my shoulder.

"I've got out at last," said I, "in spite of you and Jane! And I've pulled off most of the paper, so you can't put me back!"

Now why should that man have fainted? But he did, and right across my path by the wall, so that I had to creep over him every time!

"WHY I WROTE THE YELLOW WALLPAPER"[1]

Charlotte Perkins Gilman

MANY AND MANY a reader has asked that. When the story first
came out, in the *New England Magazine* about 1891, a Boston
physician made protest in *The Transcript*. Such a story ought not
to be written, he said; it was enough to drive anyone mad to read
it. Another physician, in Kansas I think, wrote to say that it was
the best description of incipient insanity he had ever seen, and—
begging my pardon—had I been there? Now the story of the story
is this: For many years, I suffered from a severe and continuous
nervous breakdown tending to melancholia—and beyond. During
about the third year of this trouble I went, in devout faith and some
faint stir of hope, to a noted specialist in nervous diseases, the best
known in the country. This wise man put me to bed and applied
the rest cure, to which a still good physique responded so promptly
that he concluded there was nothing much the matter with me, and
sent me home with solemn advice to "live as domestic a life as far as
possible," to "have but two hours' intellectual life a day," and "never
to touch pen, brush or pencil again as long as I lived." This was
in 1887. I went home and obeyed those directions for some three
months, and came so near to the border line of utter mental ruin
that I could see over. Then, using the remnants of intelligence that
remained, and helped by a wise friend, I cast the noted specialist's
advice to the winds and went to work again—work, the normal life
of every human being; work, in which is joy and growth and service,
without which one is a pauper and a parasite; ultimately recovering

---

1   First published in Gilman's magazine *The Forerunner,* October 1913.

some measure of power. Being naturally moved to rejoicing by this narrow escape, I wrote *The Yellow Wallpaper*, with its embellishments and additions to carry out the ideal (I never had hallucinations or objections to my mural decorations) and sent a copy to the physician who so nearly drove me mad. He never acknowledged it. The little book is valued by alienists and as a good specimen of one kind of literature. It has to my knowledge saved one woman from a similar fate—so terrifying her family that they let her out into normal activity and she recovered. But the best result is this. Many years later I was told that the great specialist had admitted to friends of his that he had altered his treatment of neurasthenia since reading *The Yellow Wallpaper*. It was not intended to drive people crazy, but to save people from being driven crazy, and it worked.

THE TWO OFFERS[1]

Frances Ellen Watkins Harper

"WHAT IS THE matter with you, Laura, this morning? I have been watching you this hour, and in that time you have commenced a half dozen letters and torn them all up. What matter of such grave moment is puzzling your dear little head, that you do not know how to decide?"

"Well, it is an important matter: I have two offers for marriage, and I do not know which to choose."

"I should accept neither, or to say the least, not at present."

"Why not?"

"Because I think a woman who is undecided between two offers, has not love enough for either to make a choice; and in that very hesitation, indecision, she has a reason to pause and seriously reflect, lest her marriage, instead of being an affinity of souls or a union of hearts, should only be a mere matter of bargain and sale, or an affair of convenience and selfish interest."

"But I consider them both very good offers, just such as many a girl would gladly receive. But to tell you the truth, I do not think that I regard either as a woman should the man she chooses for her husband. But then if I refuse, there is the risk of being an old maid, and that is not to be thought of."

"Well, suppose there is, is that the most dreadful fate that can befall a woman? Is there not more intense wretchedness in an ill-assorted marriage—more utter loneliness in a loveless home,

1   First published in two installments in 1859 in the newly founded *Anglo-African* magazine and considered the first short story in English published by a non-anonymous African American woman in the United States.

than in the lot of the old maid who accepts her earthly mission as a gift from God, and strives to walk the path of life with earnest and unfaltering steps?"

"Oh! what a little preacher you are. I really believe that you were cut out for an old maid; that when nature formed you, she put in a double portion of intellect to make up for a deficiency of love; and yet you are kind and affectionate. But I do not think that you know anything of the grand, over-mastering passion, or the deep necessity of woman's heart for loving."

"Do you think so?" resumed the first speaker; and bending over her work she quietly applied herself to the knitting that had lain neglected by her side, during this brief conversation; but as she did so, a shadow flitted over her pale and intellectual brow, a mist gathered in her eyes, and a slight quivering of the lips, revealed a depth of feeling to which her companion was a stranger.

But before I proceed with my story, let me give you a slight history of the speakers. They were cousins, who had met life under different auspices. Laura Lagrange, was the only daughter of rich and indulgent parents, who had spared no pains to make her an accomplished lady. Her cousin, Janette Alston, was the child of parents, rich only in goodness and affection. Her father had been unfortunate in business, and dying before he could retrieve his fortunes, left his business in an embarrassed state. His widow was unacquainted with his business affairs, and when the estate was settled, hungry creditors had brought their claims and the lawyers had received their fees, she found herself homeless and almost penniless, and she who had been sheltered in the warm clasp of loving arms, found them too powerless to shield her from the pitiless pelting storms of adversity. Year after year she struggled with poverty and wrestled with want, till her toil-worn hands became too feeble to hold the shattered chords of existence, and her tear-dimmed eyes grew heavy with the slumber of death. Her daughter had watched over her with untiring devotion, had closed her eyes in death, and gone out into the busy, restless world, missing a precious tone from the voices of earth, a beloved step from the paths of life. Too self reliant to depend on the charity of relations, she endeavored to support herself by her own exertions, and she had succeeded. Her path for a while was marked with struggle and trial, but instead of uselessly repining, she met them bravely, and her life became not a thing of ease and indulgence, but of conquest, victory, and accomplishments. At the time when this conversation took place, the deep trials of her life had passed away. The achievements of her genius had won her a position in the literary world, where she shone as one of its bright particular stars. And with her fame came a competence of worldly means, which gave her leisure for improvement, and the riper development of her rare talents. And she, that pale intellectual woman, whose genius gave life and vivacity to the social circle, and whose presence threw a halo of beauty and grace around the charmed atmosphere in which she moved, had at one period of her life, known the mystic and solemn strength of an all-absorbing love. Years faded into the misty past, had seen the kindling of her eye, the quick flushing of her cheek, and the wild throbbing of her heart, at tones of a voice long since hushed to the stillness of death. Deeply, wildly, passionately, she had loved. Her whole life seemed like the pouring out of rich, warm and gushing affections. This love quickened her talents, inspired her genius, and threw over her life a tender and spiritual earnestness. And then came a fearful shock, a mournful waking from that "dream of beauty and delight." A shadow fell around her path; it came between her and the object of her heart's worship; first a few cold words, estrangement, and then a painful separation; the old story of woman's pride—digging the sepulchre of her happiness, and then a new-made grave, and her path over it to the spirit world; and thus faded out from that young heart her bright, brief and saddened dream of life. Faint and spirit-broken, she turned from the scenes associated with the memory of the loved and lost. She tried to break the chain of sad associations that bound her to the mournful past; and so, pressing back the bitter sobs from her almost breaking heart, like the dying dolphin, whose beauty is born of its death anguish, her genius gathered strength from suffering and wondrous power and brilliancy from the agony she hid within the desolate chambers of her soul. Men hailed her as one of earth's strangely gifted children, and wreathed the garlands of fame for her brow, when it was throbbing with a wild and fearful unrest. They breathed her name with applause, when through the lonely halls of her stricken spirit, was an earnest cry for peace, a deep yearning for sympathy and heart-support.

But life, with its stern realities, met her; its solemn responsibilities confronted her, and turning, with an earnest and shattered spirit, to life's duties and trials, she found a calmness and strength that she had only imagined in her dreams of poetry and song. We will now pass over a period of ten years, and the cousins have met again. In that calm and lovely woman, in whose eyes is a depth of tenderness, tempering the flashes of her genius, whose looks and tones are full of sympathy and love, we recognize the once smitten and stricken Janette Alston. The bloom of her girlhood had given way to a higher type of spiritual beauty, as if some unseen hand had been polishing and refining the temple in which her lovely spirit found its habitation; and this had been the fact. Her inner life had grown beautiful, and it was this that was constantly developing the outer. Never, in the early flush of womanhood, when an absorbing love had lit up her eyes and glowed in her life, had she appeared so interesting as when, with a countenance which seemed overshadowed with a spiritual light, she bent over the death-bed of a young woman, just lingering at the shadowy gates of the unseen land.

"Has he come?" faintly but eagerly exclaimed the dying woman. "Oh! how I have longed for his coming, and even in death he forgets me."

"Oh, do not say so, dear Laura, some accident may have detained him," said Janette to her cousin; for on that bed, from whence she will never rise, lies the once-beautiful and lighthearted Laura Lagrange, the brightness of whose eyes has long since been dimmed with tears, and whose voice had become like a harp whose every chord is turned to sadness—whose faintest thrill and loudest vibrations are but the variations of agony. A heavy hand was laid upon her once warm and bounding heart, and a voice came whispering through her soul, that she must die. But, to her, the tidings was a message of deliverance—a voice, hushing her wild sorrows to the calmness of resignation and hope. Life had grown so weary upon her head—the future looked so hopeless—she had no wish to tread again the track where thorns had pierced her feet, and clouds overcast her sky; and she hailed the coming of death's angel as the footsteps of a welcome friend. And yet, earth had one object so very dear to her weary heart. It was her absent and recreant husband; for, since that conversation, she had accepted one of her offers, and become a wife. But, before she married, she learned that great lesson of human experience and woman's life, to love the man who bowed at her shrine, a willing worshipper. He had a pleasing address, raven hair, flashing eyes, a voice of thrilling sweetness, and lips of persuasive eloquence; and being well versed in the ways of the world, he won his way to her heart, and she became his bride, and he was proud of his prize. Vain and superficial in his character, he looked upon marriage not as a divine sacrament for the soul's development and human progression, but as the title-deed that gave him possession of the woman he thought he loved. But alas for her, the laxity of his principles had rendered him unworthy of the deep and undying devotion of a pure-hearted woman; but, for awhile, he hid from her his true character, and she blindly loved him, and for a short period was happy in the consciousness of being beloved; though sometimes a vague unrest would fill her soul, when, overflowing with a sense of the good, the beautiful, and the true, she would turn to him, but find no response to the deep yearnings of her soul—no appreciation of life's highest realities—its solemn grandeur and significant importance.

Their souls never met, and soon she found a void in her bosom, that his earth-born love could not fill. He did not satisfy the wants of her mental and moral nature—between him and her there was no affinity of minds, no intercommunion of souls.

Talk as you will of woman's deep capacity for loving, of the strength of her affectional nature. I do not deny it; but will the mere possession of any human love, fully satisfy all the demands of her whole being? You may paint her in poetry or fiction, as a frail vine, clinging to her brother man for support, and dying when deprived of it; and all this may sound well enough to please the imaginations of school-girls, or love-lorn maidens. But woman—the true woman—if you would render her happy, it needs more than the mere development of her affectional nature. Her conscience should be enlightened, her faith in the true and right established, scope given to her Heaven-endowed and God-given faculties. The true aim of female education should be not a development of one or two, but all the faculties of the human soul, because no perfect womanhood is developed by imperfect culture. Intense love is often akin to intense suffering, and to trust the whole wealth of a woman's nature on the frail bark of human love, may often be like trusting a cargo of gold and precious gems, to a bark that has never battled with the storm, or buffeted the waves. Is it any wonder, then, that so many life-barks go down, paving the ocean of time with precious hearts and wasted hopes? that so many float around us, shattered and dismasted wrecks? that so many are stranded on the shoals of existence, mournful beacons and solemn warnings for the thoughtless, to whom marriage is a careless and hasty rushing together of the affections? Alas that an institution so fraught with good for humanity should be so perverted, and that state of life, which should be filled with happiness, become so replete with misery. And this was the fate of Laura Lagrange. For a brief period after her marriage her life seemed like a bright and beautiful dream, full of hope and radiant with joy. And then there came a change—he found other attractions that lay beyond the pale of home influences. The gambling saloon had power to win him from her side, he had lived in an element of unhealthy and unhallowed excitements, and the society of a loving wife, the pleasures of a well-regulated home, were enjoyments too tame for one who had vitiated his tastes by the pleasures of sin. There were charmed houses of vice, built upon dead men's loves, where, amid the flow of song, laughter, wine, and careless mirth, he would spend hour after hour, forgetting the cheek that was paling through his neglect, heedless of the tear-dimmed eyes, peering anxiously into the darkness, waiting, or watching his return.

The influence of old associations was upon him. In early life, home had been to him a place of ceilings and walls, not a true home, built upon goodness, love and truth. It was a place where velvet carpets hushed its tread, where images of loveliness and beauty invoked into being by painter's art and sculptor's skill, pleased the eye and gratified the taste, where magnificence surrounded his way and costly clothing adorned his person; but it was not the place for the true culture and right development of his soul. His father had been too much engrossed in making money, and his mother in spending it, in striving to maintain a fashionable position in society, and shining in the eyes of the world, to give the proper direction to the character of their wayward and impulsive son. His mother put beautiful robes upon his body, but left ugly scars upon his soul; she pampered his appetite, but starved his spirit. Every mother should be a true artist, who knows how to weave into her child's life images of grace and beauty, the true poet capable of writing on the soul of childhood the harmony of love and truth, and teaching it how to produce the grandest of all poems—the poetry of a true and noble life. But in his home, a love for the good, the true and right, had been sacrificed at the shrine of frivolity and fashion. That parental authority which should have been preserved as a string of precious pearls, unbroken and unscattered, was simply the administration of chance. At one time obedience was enforced by authority, at another time by flattery and promises, and just as often it was not enforced at all. His early associations were formed as chance directed, and from his want of home-training, his character received a bias, his life a shade, which ran through every avenue of his existence, and darkened all his future hours. Oh, if we would trace the history of all the crimes that have o'ershadowed this sin-shrouded and sorrow-darkened world of ours, how many might be seen arising from the wrong home influences, or the weakening of the home ties. Home should always be the best school for the affections, the birthplace of high resolves, and the altar upon which lofty aspirations are kindled, from whence the soul may go forth strengthened, to act its part aright in the great drama of life with conscience enlightened, affections cultivated, and reason and judgment dominant. But alas for the young wife. Her husband had not been blessed with such a home. When he entered the arena of life, the voices from home did not linger around his path as angels of guidance about his steps; they were not like so many messages to invite him to deeds of high and holy worth. The memory of no sainted mother arose between him and deeds of darkness; the earnest prayers of no father arrested him in his downward course: and before a year of his married life had waned, his young wife had learned to wait and mourn his frequent and uncalled-for absence. More than once had she seen him come home from his midnight haunts, the bright intelligence of his eye displaced by the drunkard's stare, and his manly gait changed to the inebriate's stagger; and she was beginning to know the bitter agony that is compressed in the mournful words, a drunkard's wife. And then there came a bright but brief episode in her experience; the angel of life gave to her existence a deeper meaning and loftier significance; she sheltered in the warm clasp of her loving arms, a dear babe, a precious child, whose love filled every chamber of her heart, and felt the fount of maternal love gushing so new within her soul. That child was hers. How overshadowing was the love with which she bent over its helplessness, how much it helped to fill the void and chasms in her soul. How many lonely hours were beguiled by its winsome ways, its answering smiles and fond caresses. How exquisite and solemn was the feeling that thrilled her heart when she clasped the tiny hands together and taught her dear child to call God "Our Father."

What a blessing was that child. The father paused in his head-long career, awed by the strange beauty and precocious intellect of his child; and the mother's life had a better expression through her ministrations of love. And then there came hours of bitter anguish, shading the sunlight of her home and hushing the music of her heart. The angel of death bent over the couch of her child and bea-coned it away. Closer and closer the mother strained her child to her wildly heaving breast, and struggled with the heavy hand that lay upon its heart. Love and agony contended with death, and the language of the mother's heart was,

> "Oh, Death, away! that innocent is mine;
> I cannot spare him from my arms to lay him,
> Death, in thine. I am a mother,
> Death; I gave that darling birth
> I could not bear his lifeless limbs
> Should moulder in the earth."

But death was stronger than love and mightier than agony and won the child for the land of crystal founts and deathless flowers, and the poor, stricken mother sat down beneath the shadow of her mighty grief, feeling as if a great light had gone out from her soul, and that the sunshine had suddenly faded around her path. She turned in her deep anguish to the father of her child, the loved and cherished dead. For awhile his words were kind and tender, his heart seemed subdued, and his tenderness fell upon her worn and weary heart like rain on perishing flowers, or cooling waters to lips all parched with thirst and scorched with fever; but the change was evanescent, the influence of unhallowed associations and evil habits had vitiated and poisoned the springs of his existence. They had bound him in their meshes, and he lacked the moral strength to break his fetters, and stand erect in all the strength and dignity of a true manhood, making life's highest excellence his ideal, and striving to gain it.

And yet moments of deep contrition would sweep over him, when he would resolve to abandon the wine-cup forever, when he was ready to forswear the handling of another card, and he would try to break away from the associations that he felt were working his ruin; but when the hour of temptation came his strength was weakness, his earnest purposes were cobwebs, his well-meant resolutions ropes of sand, and thus passed year after year of the married life of Laura Lagrange. She tried to hide her agony from the public gaze, to smile when her heart was almost breaking. But year after year her voice grew fainter and sadder, her once light and bounding step grew slower and faltering. Year after year she wrestled with agony, and strove with despair, till the quick eyes of her brother read, in the paling of her cheek and the dimming eye, the secret anguish of her worn and weary spirit. On that wan, sad face, he saw the death-tokens, and he knew the dark wing of the mystic angel swept coldly around her path. "Laura," said her brother to her one day, "you are not well, and I think you need our mother's tender care and nursing. You are daily losing strength, and if you will go I will accompany you." At first, she hesitated, she shrank almost instinctively from presenting that pale sad face to the loved ones at home. That face was such a telltale; it told of heart-sickness, of hope deferred, and the mournful story of unrequited love. But then a deep yearning for home sympathy woke within her a passionate longing for love's kind words, for tenderness and heart-support, and she resolved to seek the home of her childhood and lay her weary head upon her mother's bosom, to be folded again in her loving arms, to lay that poor, bruised and aching heart where it might beat and throb closely to the loved ones at home. A kind welcome awaited her. All that love and tenderness could devise was done to bring the bloom to her cheek and the light to her eye; but it was all in vain; hers was a disease that no medicine could cure, no earthly balm would heal. It was a slow wasting of the vital forces, the sickness of the soul. The unkindness and neglect of her husband, lay like a leaden weight upon her heart, and slowly oozed way its life-drops. And where was he that had won her love, and then cast it aside as a useless thing, who rifled her heart of its wealth and spread bitter ashes upon its broken altars? He was lingering away from her when the death-damps were gathering on her brow, when his name was trembling on her lips! lingering away! when she was watching his coming, though the death films were gathering before her eyes, and earthly things were fading from her vision. "I think I hear him now," said the dying woman, "surely that is his step;" but the sound died away in the distance. Again she started from an uneasy slumber, "that is his voice! I am so glad he has come." Tears gathered in the eyes of the sad watchers by that dying bed, for they knew that she was deceived. He had not returned. For her sake they wished his coming. Slowly the hours waned away, and then came the sad, soul-sickening thought that she was forgotten, forgotten in the last hour of human need, forgotten when the spirit, about to be dissolved, paused for the last time on the threshold of existence, a weary watcher at the gates of death. "He has forgotten me," again she faintly murmured, and the last tears she would ever shed on earth sprung to her mournful eyes, and clasping her hands together in silent anguish, a few broken sentences issued from her pale and quivering lips. They were prayers for strength and earnest pleading for him who had desolated her young life, by turning its sunshine to shadows, its smiles to tears. "He has forgotten me," she murmured again, "but I can bear it, the bitterness of death is passed, and soon I hope to exchange the shadows of death for the brightness of eternity, the rugged paths of life for the golden streets of glory, and the care and turmoils of earth for the peace and rest of heaven." Her voice grew fainter and fainter, they saw the shadows that never deceive flit over her pale and faded face, and knew that the death angel waited to soothe their weary one to rest, to calm the throbbing of her bosom and cool the fever of her brain. And amid the silent hush of their grief the freed spirit, refined through suffering, and brought into divine harmony through the spirit of the living Christ, passed over the dark waters of death as on a bridge of light, over whose radiant arches hovering angels bent. They parted the dark locks from her marble brow, closed the waxen lids over the once bright and laughing eye, and left her to the dreamless slumber of the grave. Her cousin turned from that death-bed a sadder and wiser woman. She resolved more earnestly than ever to make the world better by her example, gladder by her presence, and to kindle the fires of her genius on the altars of universal love and truth. She had a higher and better object in all her writings than the mere acquisition of gold, or acquirement of fame. She felt that she had a high and holy mission on the battle-field of existence, that life was not given her to be frittered away in nonsense, or wasted away in trifling pursuits. She would willingly espouse an unpopular cause but not an unrighteous one. In her the down-trodden slave found an earnest advocate; the flying fugitive remembered her kindness as he stepped cautiously through our Republic, to gain his freedom in a monarchial land, having broken the chains on which the rust of centuries had gathered. Little children learned to name her with affection, the poor called her blessed, as she broke her bread to the pale lips of hunger. Her life was like a beautiful story, only it was clothed with the dignity of reality and invested with the sublimity of truth. True, she was an old maid. No husband brightened her life with his love, or shaded it with his neglect. No children nestling lovingly in her arms called her mother. No one appended Mrs. to her name; she was indeed an old maid, not vainly striving to keep up an appearance of girlishness, when departed was written on her youth. Not vainly pining at her loneliness and isolation: the world was full of warm, loving hearts, and her own beat in unison with them. Neither was she always sentimentally sighing for something to love, objects of affection were all around her, and the world was not so wealthy in love that it had no use for hers; in blessing others she made a life and benediction, and as old age descended peacefully and gently upon her, she had learned one of life's most precious lessons, that true happiness consists not so much in the fruition of our wishes as in the regulation of desires and the full development and right culture of our whole natures.

THE PRESCRIPTION[1]

Elizabeth Stoddard

THE DOCTOR SAID that change of air would do me good, and that the farther I went from home the better. It would be wise to go, he thought, beyond the reach of daily newspapers and Adams Express; an irregular mail would be advisable. "Choose a village," he added, "where there is no railroad, no telegraph wires, no barrack hotel, and no Gothic meeting-house."

"How long must she stay?" my husband asked.

The Doctor eyed him a moment, as if a reply was rising in his mind which he would like to give utterance to, but had a doubt whether it was best to do so. He answered presently, that I must stay out of the city till I was in a different condition from the one I was in at present.

When this conversation happened on a summer afternoon in my chamber, a torn Zouave jacket of white Marseilles was lying on the sofa where the Doctor sat. A few minutes before his arrival my husband, Gérard Fuller, entered the room and came to the table where I was drawing, and being very tall and very near-sighted bent his head over my shoulder; the gleam of the gilt buttons on the said jacket, which I had on, must have caught his eye, for he started back with the exclamation:

"Haven't I told you never to wear these things? Fast women only should wear them."

Before I could put my pencil down he cut the jacket open with

1   First published in Harper's *New Monthly Magazine* 28 (December 1864): 794–800.

his penknife, pulled it from my arms, tore it across and tossed it over on the sofa. I replaced it with a drab-colored barége, and seated myself at a distance from the table where Gérard stood contemplating my sketch, to await further demonstration from him, when a rap came on the door and the Doctor bustled in. It is possible that there might have been an unusual expression in our faces, for he only gave a queer "hem," and referred to his memorandum-book. After perusing it a while he remarked that he had been looking over, in his carriage, a clever little book by a Frenchman, who said, "that a woman may be loved for three things: for her superior intellect—a love serious but rare; for her beauty—a love vulgar and brief; for the qualities of her heart—a love lasting but monotonous." His eyes then dropped on the torn jacket, and without waiting for any comment on his quotation he asked me how I felt, and proposed change of air for me.

"Milk-and-water will be good for her, I suppose, in the out-of-the-way place you suggest," continued Gérard.

"Unless she finds the milk of human kindness there," the Doctor replied.

"Good, Doctor, but said by Grimaldi thirty years ago; and I believe he added something about the cream of the joke."

"I dare say. Mrs. Fuller," and the Doctor turned toward me, putting his fingers on my wrist, "when can you leave home?"

Gérard answered hastily that I could go any day, but he could not accompany me. Gérard is a cloth importer, and mid-summer is his busiest time; the Doctor knew this fact.

"I sent a patient," he said, "two years ago to a little town famous for its bad air, its disagreeable scenery, and the stupidity of its inhabitants. I wish you would allow your wife to go there" (here his eyes rested on the jacket again). "I am sure she can get in the same house where my patient boarded; and if you say so, I will write to my old friend, John Bowman, ancient mariner, who lives in it, and engage a room."

"Oh," said Gérard, in his roughest way, "I do not believe it is necessary to write your friend; he will be glad to take a boarder, and Caroline can go to-morrow if she chooses."

"Just so," answered the Doctor, rising. "It is understood then, Mrs. Fuller, that you will follow my directions."

"You had better make them more explicit," I answered.

"I'll drop in to-morrow to see how you are, and give you my final say."

"Where is that happy village?" inquired Gérard.

"Eighteen miles from the small city of Berford, on the sea-coast; its name is Marlow. Good-day."

Gérard left me immediately, and, naturally, I looked in the glass as soon as I was alone. I saw no difference in my appearance, and could not account for the Doctor's penetration; for I was convinced that he knew Gérard had torn off the jacket from me. Upon second thought, I remembered that he had shown the same manner once before. It was when Gérard happened to come home one day, in the beginning of my illness, with a carriage, to take me out with him. The Doctor, perceiving that I did not wish to go, said that I had better stay at home that day. Gérard flung about in wrath, and finally rushed out of the room and went off with the carriage. The Doctor asked me, suddenly, if I was nervous before I was married. "No," I said.

"Your grandmother," he remarked, "must be an old muff."

As Gérard had said the same thing frequently of her, I supposed it must be true that she was; but I was impressed with an idea that the Doctor had a different reason for thinking so from what Gérard had. I was not left alone much, was I? the Doctor questioned. What individual tastes or employments had I? Did I ever feel hemmed in by circumstances? He had often noticed that dyspeptic people felt that way. These, with many more strange questions, he asked, and I believe I answered him coherently, though, while I think of it now, I wonder that I was not embarrassed.

He came the next day after the episode of the jacket, and told me that he had already written to Mr. Bowman, who would be ready to receive me as soon as the letter reached him. He also gave me a prescription in a sealed envelope, adding that I need not open it till I had arrived in Marlow, for there was an apothecary's shop there.

"The Doctor has left nothing for me to arrange, I conclude," said Gérard, when he returned home that evening.

"He has even provided for me after I get there, in giving me a sealed prescription."

"Give it to me at once."

I offered it to him in silence.

"Take it," he said, after looking at it a moment; "do you imagine I wish to break the seal?"

I did imagine it, but did not say so.

"You will obey him, of course?"

"Shall I not?"

He shrugged his shoulders for reply.

It was several days before my traveling-dress came home and I was ready to go. Gérard continually wondered why the Doctor did not come to pack my trunk and order a carriage. He also begged me not to indulge in any sentimental twaddle on his account; which was entirely satirical on his part—for I never indulged in any thing of the kind in regard to him—and endeavored to torment me after the old fashion. He remained at home the day of my departure, but said little. He appeared interested in a novel, but I noticed that he was not so absorbed in it as to prevent his following me over the house, pursuing me from room to room with his book in his hand. He filled my purse, and a new carpet-bag was silently presented to me with various useful nicknacks in it, for which I expressed my gratitude. He accompanied me to the boat, and we had the pleasure of looking out from the opposite windows of the carriage on the drive thither. Depositing my carpet-bag and shawl on the cabin floor, he obtained a chair for me, and then stood before me in a rigid attitude. I untied my bonnet, pinned it to a berth curtain, took off my gloves, and fanned myself. He stared at my hands, oblivious of the crowd of people who hurried to and fro past us, till a man cried out, "All ashore that's going!" He pushed away my fan then, and whispered,

"It's a pity we are married."

In lieu of a reply I fanned myself with violence, for I did not know what reply to make.

"I love you, and I am tired of you; you fatigue me."

I fanned on.

"I wish the devil had that fan."

I shut it up. "Do you think it would cool him, Gérard?"

"Placid wit!"

"I am afraid the boat will start."

"Of course you are. I am going. Won't you say any thing?—send a message to your grandmother?"

I put out my hand without a word; he grasped it till I nearly cried out with pain, and was gone.

Before I had time to start a train of reflection upon the novelty of my situation the boat started; the stewardess put a bit of paper in my hand marked "37," and informed me that it was my berth; the Captain, perambulating the cabin, stopped and asked me if I would go down to supper; and a lady, with a cushion in a leather strap, asked me to exchange berths with her, as she preferred mine to hers. By this time the boat was rocking unpleasantly, my head ached, and I was glad to retire to "35" having at once given up 37 to the lady of the cushion. At sunrise we arrived in port. A train was waiting to convey passengers to different towns by a circuitous route. At the Berford station I alighted, and discovering there the Marlow mail wagon took passage therein.

"Mr. Bowman told me to look out for a lady," said the driver, "and I expect you are the invalid, or convalescent, or something of that sort boarder, ain't you?"

Somehow I felt that I had suddenly lost the claim to invalidism, and so I said that I was a convalescent.

"The air is strong in Marlow," he continued, "and no mistake; it kills or cures strangers. Mostly kills the folks that live there, too, before they get to old age. Old Bowman, though, is seventy; he's tough. Ever introduced to him? He is a first-rate man, and no mistake; he'll do what's right by you. As for myself, speaking of health, I am twenty-four, and I have had typhus fever, dysentery, inflammatory rheumatism, and no end of stoppages; but I calculate to enjoy myself for all that."

His loquacity continued and amused me till we reached John Bowman's house.

"There he is," said the driver, "a walking up and down in the sun."

"Hi yi!" said the old man, when the driver stopped; "have you brought somebody here, Ike?"

"That ere boarder, you know."

He approached the wagon, and lifting a white beaver hat, said: "Your servant, marm."

"Bear a hand, will you, said the driver, "and unlash the trunk?"

Mr. Bowman propped his gold-headed cane against the paling, turned up the cuffs of his blue cloth jacket, and proceeded to unfasten the trunk. I observed that, in spite of his handsome beaver hat and gold-headed cane, he wore coarse gray trowsers, patched at the knees, and cow-hide shoes; and that he had a noble head, pale, dignified features, long gray hair rising from his forehead like a crown, and a diminutive figure. He interested me, and I felt no surprise at the fact of his being a friend of Doctor Brown's. I looked at the house before I entered it. It had been long built, and never painted; the martins were flying round the squat chimneys; and on the ridge-pole of the low porch several pigeons were daintily stepping to and fro. There was an iron knocker on the door, and before it a brick pavement, in the cracks of which tufts and seams of grass grew. The house interested me also.

"Now, then," said Mr. Bowman, smiting the dust from his hands, "we are ready, marm. Will you walk in? Mrs. Bowman's dinner is ready."

He opened the door softly, and preceding me, entered a room, where a tall, Roman-nosed old lady sat reading a green flannel-covered book, which I found afterward was Baxter's "Saint's Rest." Mr. Bowman waved his hand and said, "This is she;" and Mrs. Bowman rose, addressing me with a few precise words.

"Dinner, mother," he interrupted her with.

"Don't be impatient, father; let her get her things off."

He took my bonnet and shawl away, and placed me at the table. Mrs. Bowman went out, and returned with two covered dishes and a tea-pot, and we began dinner. She conversed during the meal; but her husband was silent for the most part, with the exception of a few "yi-hi's" and "pooh-pooh's," which did not seem to produce much effect upon her.

"What is the nature of your complaint?" she asked.

" Her complaint is going so fast she can't recall its name," he said.

"Father is so confident always," she remarked, with a smile of pity.

"Pooh! nonsense, mother."

"You remember what the Psalmist says, father?"

For answer he buried his face in a large mug which contained cold coffee, his constant drink, and draining it, rose from the table with twinkling eyes and went out. She gave a smiling sigh of superiority as he disappeared, and proceeded in a deliberate way to clear the table. I became interested in her performances, and declined her proposal that I should go to bed till tea-time. The remains of the dinner she disposed of in various bowls, and carried to the "cellar-way" to keep cool. She also prepared a hash for supper, and washed the dishes. I followed her into the kitchen to witness the final touch at her mid-day work, which was to scour the hooks and trammels which were already hanging on the crane as bright as steel. All this made me unmindful of the lapse of time, and I was surprised when Mr. Bowman came back with the announcement that it was going on for five o'clock.

"Hasn't she been up stairs yet, mother?" he exclaimed.

"No," she answered; "she said she was not tired."

"I will go now, Mr. Bowman, if you will show me the way," I said.

"I hope you won't mind the smell of the sea-weed when the tide is out," Mrs. Bowman remarked.

The tide! What could that have to do with my going up stairs? I remembered catching a glimpse of a bay as we turned into the street where the house was situated, but there was no view of it in front.

"Nothing would tempt me," she continued, "to do my work or to stay in the back part of this house; but it is father's whim to stay here, with the butment all crumbled away, and he will stay till the underpinning goes."

He thumped the floor gently with his cane to attract my attention, and said:

''She's here for sea-weed, and the creek, and all. Don't Doctor Brown know what he is about, mother?"

He opened the door before she could reply, and I followed him. The stairs dividing on a platform about midway, we turned to the left, went up a few steps into a narrow passage, at the end of which was a door painted light blue. It was the door of my room.

"You'll like it, he said, as we entered, "because there is such a prospect from the window. It will do you good. *I* look out of it at odd times, and my mind goes out on my old voyages to Amsterdam, Leghorn, and Liverpool. I think you will like the prospect, I say."

I looked from the open window.

"Why, Mr. Bowman," I exclaimed, "your house is built on the sand!"

"Isn't it?" he chuckled, "and the floods don't wash it away either. Put your head out; streets in front of the house, seas behind; was there ever such a situation besides?"

I put my head out, and obtained a novel view. The house stood on the upper end of a marsh, half of its foundation on the border of it, and half on the solid ground of the street. A wide creek flowed past the underpinning of piles, whose channel had been divested by the "butment" now crumbling apart, but which still kept the creek from making further inroads into the spongy yards of the neighbors who lived higher up the street. Below the creek stretched the beautiful bay of Marlow, and beyond that rolled the ocean, over which Mr. Bowman's mind went on his old voyages.

"This is almost Venetian, Mr. Bowman; colorless Venice without architecture."

"I never went there; they have strange craft in that place I am told; the natives paddle their boats under the girls' windows. I went to St. Petersburg once, in the time of the Emperor Paul. Nothing will disturb you here, unless Gil Jones comes up in his punt at high tide to steal oysters. You'll hear the water splash sometimes; that's pleasant."

I must have looked tired or abstracted, for he made a hasty exit on tip-toe, without another word. I was weary; the sight of my unpacked trunk was discouraging. How could Gérard have allowed me to leave home alone? What occupation was I to find in this queer, lonely house with these strange, lonely old people?

After tea I unlocked my trunk, shook out my dresses, and looked over my stock of fineries. All at once I felt in better spirits; my clothes seemed to belong to me more than they had for a long time, and a strange sense of freedom stole over me when I recollected that I could keep the candle burning as long as I pleased, and sit up all night if I saw fit.

A sheet of dull, unbroken light hung before the shutterless window when I woke next morning. A mild silvery mist hid land and sea; immediately beneath the window I could see little pools of black water, and a bed of stones covered with a web of green viscous weeds. The tide was out. A faint breeze touched my face with dampness when I raised the sash, and a cloud of delicate mist edged itself into the room.

How different it was at noon!

Mr. Bowman was going across the bay to fish and so we dined early; by twelve o'clock he was hoisting sail at the one wharf Marlow could boast of. Mrs. Bowman went to a funeral several miles distant, and the house was left to me.

I shut the windows below, bolted the outside doors, and betook myself to my room. Outside there was no shade, the pale marsh grass scorched in the sun, and the beach glittered as if every pebble was a precious stone. The water along the shore and at the mouth of the creek lay still and white, untouched by the breeze which ruffled the waters of the bay; its outlet spreading under the horizon was smooth and white also. It allured me like a magic mirror. If I should look steadfastly at it some strange mystery would be revealed to me.

It occurred to me while I stood gazing seaward to get the doctor's prescription. I opened the envelope and found on a bit of paper the following words:

"Comprehend yourself, then you will be able to comprehend others; to do this is necessary in your case."

My case! Was it pictured in yonder magic mirror and so reflected upon my mind, or were my mental eyes opening at last?

I passed several days in thinking that I was deep in thought, but I was simply in a chaos of feeling which made my brain turbid. I sat much by my window, and continually dropped into vague emotional dreams which produced as apparently a purposeless and futile agitation in my mind as the wind produces on the sea, stirring it up within its limits, but not able to move it an inch beyond. But the chaos was a process I was unaware of till it was completed by slight influences independent of my own will. One evening a tempest came up from the north, and I staid down stairs with the old people. For the most part we were silent, but as its lulls grew longer Mr. Bowman raised his voice, and his wife removed her finger from the place in the green flannel-covered book. When the tempest ceased, and all sounds had died away in the darkness of night, she remarked that she must take in the tubs she had put out to catch rain-water, and go round the house to wipe up the puddles that had leaked in.

"You are gaining, my dear," said Mr. Bowman, when she had gone.

"What am I gaining?"

"That is the secret of the sea. I knew you would go on just so, if you had the chance. I hadn't when I was young. I went hither and thither, on this voyage and that, doing the business of other men; do you think I minded what *I* was doing, hi yi? No, I didn't look into the sea, and the sea didn't look into me; but when the time of action was past, when my owners wanted younger captains and I sat me down here, my ships gone, my crews gone, then I looked into the sea, and the sea looked into me, and I learned what it is to live—late to be sure. You are alone for the first time in your life, I take it, for you are a young thing, and you are gaining. I knew you would like the prospect. Mother can't bear it; there's nothing of Baxter in it."

He laughed so loud that she was drawn back to the room to inquire if he had hysterics. I went to my room smiling too, but I felt as if there were tears in his eyes, for they were rising more pleasant, rare times though, when he asked, in mine. A band of moonlight crossed the floor, a portion of that which crossed the sea, and shimmered in long lines to the verge of the horizon.

"It is true," I reflected, "that I have been living and not thinking; nineteen years of unconscious doing what I have been directed to do. My biography is short, comprised in two facts. I lived with grandmother, and married Gérard Fuller; there is little need to look into the sea in order to expatiate on these topics. But the sea looks into me, and reminds me of my eight months of married life. There is little to account for before that. We have always known Gérard; he is thirty years old; I remember him a grown man when I was a little girl—I always had to mind him. Grandmother wished me to marry him because he is the son of her old friend, for whom she still wears a mourning ring. Gérard was the only man ever intimate at our house. He was devoted to her, though she sometimes quarreled with him. He worried her into a consent to our marriage against her judgment, for she had a theory that a woman should not be married till she was twenty-five. We had not been married a month before he told me that he wished I had her character, and wondered if my marriage had really arrested my development. From that moment I felt myself the automaton he believed me to be. He began a series of experiments with me, ranging from the lively to the severe, always ending in the severe. I never retaliated, never showed anger, never remonstrated; I have more than once endeavored to pacify him, and have shaped my course entirely by his demands. His first experiment was melodramatic. His own friend, Ned Conover, happened to admire the way my hair was arranged one day. He had hardly left us when Gérard took my comb out, and pulled out the hairpins, saying that he could not bear the way my hair was dressed. I remarked that he was hurting me, he replied that, as I was not thick-skinned, he did not believe it. But when he came home the next evening and saw that I had dressed my hair another way, he scowled and did not address a word to me for twenty-four hours. We were living with grandmother then, and I mentioned the incident to her; she looked aghast, but said nothing. Soon afterward he bought a house, and furnished it without consulting me: he supposed, he observed, that my tastes were the same as his, and that need not trouble me. Grandmother was disappointed at our leaving her; but Gérard said that young people had better be by themselves, and she made no objection. She had several skirmishes with him, however, before we moved, and I was glad when the time came for us to go. He did not alter his behavior toward me when we lived alone. He was away from home more than formerly. Sometimes when he returned there was an inquiring expression in his face; he always went away again immediately when he wore that expression. There were times more pleasant, rare times though, when he asked me to read to him while he smoked in my chamber; I never took my eyes from my book that I did not find him perusing my face with a strange intentness. When he took me to the opera, and forgot almost that I was his wife, or to the theatre, where we could not fail to have the same chord of appreciation struck. Two months ago my health began to decline. Gérard said it was the coffee, and ordered tea for breakfast; but I did not improve. Then he said it was because I read too much, and I stopped reading. It must be sewing, he concluded, want of exercise, air, and fifty other things. But I grew worse, and Doctor Brown was called. He said little at first, and the medicine he gave was so mild that I am inclined to think it was sweetened water. Gérard stormed at him, maligned him, but succumbed to all he proposed; indeed, he carried out his directions with nervous haste. He watched me more closely than ever; how many times have I opened my eyes to see his face close to mine, full of eager anxiety! But how sullen he was if I spoke to him! At last I kept my eyes shut when I knew he bent over my pillow. It was irksome to suffer this espionage. Was it wise?"

The moon was setting behind the light-house across the bay, and the sea darkened. Whether I had been wise or foolish, it was time to go to bed.

The day after the tempest Mr. Bowman handed me a letter from Gérard.

"What has Brown's prescription done for you?" it abruptly opened with. "You are impatient to return, I know; but why should you be? You have the society that always suffices you—yourself."

I laid the letter aside without finishing it. "He is a brute," I said; "let me be free of him. I am free."

"Mr. Bowman," I said, when I want down stairs, "men are brutes."

"Yes, my dear, except when women tyrannize over them."

"What are they then, father?" his wife asked.

"Transformed into meek angels and saints. But why do you say so now particularly, my dear; did you hear me swearing at mother?"

"The old story-books on the shelves in the passage say so."

"So they do, my dear; hi yi, those stories went on more than one voyage with me."

"Poor kind of bread to cast on the waters, father," Mrs. Bowman observed.

"It returned though."

I left them arguing the point. It was evident that she did not consider Mr. Bowman one of the saved; but I knew that she thought him one of the wisest of men, and was happy with him.

I determined not to answer Gérard.

Within a week after the arrival of the letter I received one from Doctor Brown, which was more pithy even than Gérard's. It contained the following advice:

> "Pursue your studies; I am inclined to believe that my prescription was a happy one. Let me know how you are. Physicians love intricate cases; besides, an account of the Bowmans will not come amiss. Is Bowman satisfied with your progress? If he is, I shall be. Be sure to stay till the September rains come on."

I divined that Gérard had applied to the Doctor to write me, and decided not to answer the second letter also. But the two letters stirred my impulses: I began to wish the monotony of my life broken into by something tangible. I opened my portfolio, desiring to write to somebody, but what correspondent could I appeal to? I must write to myself—would start a Diary. I commenced at once, with a motto, of course:

> "Seldom should the morning's gold
> On the waters be unrolled;
> Or the troubled queen of night
> Lift her misty veil of light.

Neither wholly dark nor bright,
Gray by day and gray by night,
That's the light, the sky for me,
By the margent of the sea."

(Page first.)

The above motto is singularly inappropriate. It was in the vivid sunshine and clear moonlight which reigned over the sea that I tried to render the thoughts to the sea which it gave. In its light I saw images—not fantastic, airy shapes—but those of a plain man and woman named Gérard and Caroline. When will—

(Interruption.)

(Resume.)

Mr. Bowman came in to ask me to walk in the best street of Marlow, which has two rows of linden trees, short, thick, and vigorous in growth, in spite of the sea-wind, which gives them in infancy a slight slant to the northwest. Was glad to get back to my beloved Diary. How delightful it is to be able to express one's thoughts freely!

(Third page.)

I choose a new leaf each time I return to my Diary, because I do not feel that I have made a right beginning. I long to say something which is really important, and should never be seen by human eye. Some days have passed since I last wrote here. We have had rainy, dull weather. I staid down stairs, and sewed on Mrs. Bowman's patch-work, of the "Job's trouble" pattern, in red, yellow, and white calico. She has promised it for my bed next summer. Next summer! Shall I revisit these haunts again?

To-day it is clear, and Mr. Bowman is going to take me across the harbor in the *Polly*. What if I should be drowned? I think Gérard—

When we came back from our sail who should I see walking up and down the wharf but Gérard?

"Who upon 'arth is that?" queried Mr. Bowman.

"It looks like my husband."

"We are going to have a rush of strangers in Marlow," he said, embarrassed at his own surprise at the unexpected appearance of my husband. As the boat grated against the side of the wharf he stepped on the cap log, and extended his hand for the rope, which Mr. Bowman tossed toward him with, "Your servant, Sir; we are all right."

As Gérard turned it round a post he looked down at me with a curious expression, which indicated that he would wait for me to make a move, although he doubted whether I could do any thing original under his eye. Outwardly I was as calm as the water round the wharf, inwardly in a whirl. I contrived, however, by the time I put my foot on the gunwale to disentangle one idea, and that was, to take no pains to conceal the character of the relation between us, just as he was should he appear, as far as it lay in me to allow the truth to become apparent. I therefore took his hand to assist myself ashore, and dropped it immediately to walk in advance of him. Half-way up the wharf Mr. Bowman overtook me, and walked nimbly beside me with his basket of fish, while Gérard lingered behind, looking to the right and the left in admiration of the landscape.

"Does he read the 'Saint's Rest?'" Mr. Bowman slyly whispered. I shook my head, and the old man looked puzzled.

"For form's sake, Caroline," growled Gérard, on the other side, "you had better introduce me to your fisherman."

"For form's sake, Mr. Bowman, I introduce you to Mr. Fuller, but you already know him."

Gérard looked suspicious at me.

"No occasion for an introduction," Mr. Bowman answered; "I knew him from his resemblance to you."

"Is it so striking?" I laughed, scanning Gérard with a nonchalant air, and meeting his eyes, which were filled with astonishment and a certain expression which disturbed me, for it denoted approbation! He started a lively conversation on fish, which lasted till we reached our door. A large valise on the step met my view, and led my thoughts to speculate on the length of his stay. He must have come with an intention to remain. He seemed to understand my thoughts; for as we went in he said, with a meaning smile,

"You know how fond I am of fishing."

"It is too late in the season for that," I answered.

"Walk in, Sir," said Mr. Bowman. "This is my wife. Supper, mother."

For a wonder Mrs. Bowman was reading a pictorial newspaper, which served Gérard for a topic of talk with her. She grew lively in his presence. I saw at once that she would side with him if any contention should appear. I looked at Mr. Bowman, and detected a shade of sadness in his face. That he would sympathize with me I was sure. I put my hand on his brown fist as it lay beside his plate like a lump of brown bread. "My dear," he answered, with vivacity, "you are not well enough to go home yet."

"I am not going home."

Gérard raised his eyebrows.

"Father not having any children of his own alive is fond of young folks," Mrs. Bowman remarked.

"Yes," he replied, simply, "I love Mrs. Fuller."

"Don't you love children, ma'am?" Gérard asked, with some sharpness.

"I have been a mother."

"Do you love them, Gérard?" I asked, under my breath.

"Yes, but not the childish."

Had the sea told me all it might have told me? Or had it revealed but a one-sided story?

I slipped up stairs while he was engaged with the subject of the herring-fishery, and in my room saw the large valise again—the precursor of the coming of my lord and master. I took up my Diary and wrote in large letters the date of Gérard's arrival and these words—

"End of my Diary."

I then seated myself by the window. A breeze had sprung up

since sunset, and the waves were lifting up their many voices in a melancholy dirge. The moon was not up, the stars were few, and the bay was hemmed in with darkness.

I heard Gérard's quick step along the passage; he opened the door.

"Shut that window," were his words.

For reply I put my head tolerably far outside of it. After a moment's silence he began to unpack his valise, and laid out on the chairs a stock of shirts, handkerchiefs, and collars. He also approached my little table with an apparatus for shaving. The Diary caught his eye, and he deliberately read it.

"Equal to Miss Julia Mills's Diary," he commented. "But why do you end it?"

"Because you have come and would read whatever I might write."

He came toward me and offered his hand.

"Pooh, Gérard! what nonsense it is for me to take your hand."

He was silent again for a moment, and then ordered me once more to shut the window. It was damp, but I rose and left it open. As I walked across the room the impulse seized me to leave it to him; but he anticipated my thought, and caught me just as I put my hand on the latch.

"I dare say you will keep me here," I said, "but what will my staying avail you?"

"You are my wife; why shouldn't I compel you to stay?" and he favored me with Petruchio's opinion:

> "She is my goods, my chattels, she is my house,
> My household stuff, my field, my barn,
> My horse, my ox, my ass, my any thing."

"He forgot to say aught about the *soul* of the shrew, didn't he?"

Cool enough to quote Shakspeare as he was, I saw that he was deeply agitated. I went on:

"Do you know that facts are no longer stubborn to me? I shall fight them, and conquer."

"What do you mean?"

"I mean there shall be something ideal in my life to live for—an ideal man, maybe."

"Where will you find him?"

"Yonder," I answered vaguely, looking toward the window.

"Did you ever have an ideal, Caroline, that you were disappointed in utterly?"

I never had, I said, but his question disturbed me. What if I were in fault somehow?

"Madam, I will leave you. There seems to be a lack of sofas in the house for one to sleep on, but I think I can manage the night."

"Before you go, let me give you a text to discourse upon. Doctor Brown sent me from under your tyranny."

"The tyranny of love," he said to himself.

"You nearly extinguished me."

"Did I?"

"I can't love you in your way."

"No?"

"And you wouldn't let me love in my way."

"Had you any way?"

"I might have had."

He darted out like an arrow, and I fell to crying.

When I opened my door the next morning he was beside it, leaning against the wall, very pale. My impulse was to stop; but I did not follow it, and walked down stairs. We entered the room, however, at the same time. Mr. Bowman looked at me over his spectacles till I felt uncomfortable; but he was uncommonly "chipper," to use his own expression, during breakfast.

The day ended as it began. Several days passed like it. I watched Gérard, and he watched me. It was strange, but I was obliged to acknowledge that I was making his acquaintance in this silent way. He was not the man I had known as my husband. His eyes often sought mine; perhaps he was making the same mental comments.

Mr. Bowman informed us one day that he was on the point of being very sick, and begged us to take care of him. I asked him what the matter was. He replied that the foolishness of two young people of his acquaintance was killing him by inches.

I believe I turned pale and looked weak; for Gérard dropped the book he was reading, and rushed toward me, exclaiming:

"It is not you who are foolish, Caroline; it is I!"

"No, it is not you, Gérard; it is me."

"Can you love a brute?"

"Brute!" Mr. Bowman exclaimed. "She knows the universal truth that Nature did not turn us out handsomely; reptile and four-legged rudiments cling to us yet."

"Caroline!"

"Gérard!"

"Now isn't this enough to make me down sick?" cried the old man. "Kiss each other and do better, and give my love to Brown."

Gérard told me afterward, with a queer smile, that his first night in Marlow was spent in looking for my "ideal man."

"And you found him," I answered.

THE STORY OF AN HOUR[1]

Kate Chopin

KNOWING THAT MRS. Mallard was afflicted with a heart trouble, great care was taken to break to her as gently as possible the news of her husband's death.

It was her sister Josephine who told her, in broken sentences; veiled hints that revealed in half concealing. Her husband's friend Richards was there, too, near her. It was he who had been in the newspaper office when intelligence of the railroad disaster was received, with Brently Mallard's name leading the list of "killed." He had only taken the time to assure himself of its truth by a second telegram, and had hastened to forestall any less careful, less tender friend in bearing the sad message.

She did not hear the story as many women have heard the same, with a paralyzed inability to accept its significance. She wept at once, with sudden, wild abandonment, in her sister's arms. When the storm of grief had spent itself she went away to her room alone. She would have no one follow her.

There stood, facing the open window, a comfortable, roomy armchair. Into this she sank, pressed down by a physical exhaustion that haunted her body and seemed to reach into her soul.

She could see in the open square before her house the tops of trees that were all aquiver with the new spring life. The delicious breath of rain was in the air. In the street below a peddler was crying his wares. The notes of a distant song which some one was

---

1   Originally published in *Vogue* on December 6, 1894, as "The Dream of an Hour." It was later reprinted in *St. Louis Life* on January 5, 1895, as "The Story of an Hour."

singing reached her faintly, and countless sparrows were twittering in the eaves. There were patches of blue sky showing here and there through the clouds that had met and piled one above the other in the west facing her window.

She sat with her head thrown back upon the cushion of the chair, quite motionless, except when a sob came up into her throat and shook her, as a child who has cried itself to sleep continues to sob in its dreams.

She was young, with a fair, calm face, whose lines bespoke repression and even a certain strength. But now there was a dull stare in her eyes, whose gaze was fixed away off yonder on one of those patches of blue sky. It was not a glance of reflection, but rather indicated a suspension of intelligent thought.

There was something coming to her and she was waiting for it, fearfully. What was it? She did not know; it was too subtle and elusive to name. But she felt it, creeping out of the sky, reaching toward her through the sounds, the scents, the color that filled the air.

Now her bosom rose and fell tumultuously. She was beginning to recognize this thing that was approaching to possess her, and she was striving to beat it back with her will—as powerless as her two white slender hands would have been.

When she abandoned herself a little whispered word escaped her slightly parted lips. She said it over and over under her breath: "free, free, free!" The vacant stare and the look of terror that had followed it went from her eyes. They stayed keen and bright. Her pulses beat fast, and the coursing blood warmed and relaxed every inch of her body.

She did not stop to ask if it were or were not a monstrous joy that held her. A clear and exalted perception enabled her to dismiss the suggestion as trivial.

She knew that she would weep again when she saw the kind, tender hands folded in death; the face that had never looked save with love upon her, fixed and gray and dead. But she saw beyond that bitter moment a long procession of years to come that would belong to her absolutely. And she opened and spread her arms out to them in welcome. There would be no one to live for her during those coming years; she would live for herself.

There would be no powerful will bending hers in that blind persistence with which men and women believe they have a right to impose a private will upon a fellow-creature. A kind intention or a cruel intention made the act seem no less a crime as she looked upon it in that brief moment of illumination.

And yet she had loved him—sometimes. Often she had not. What did it matter! What could love, the unsolved mystery, count for in face of this possession of self-assertion which she suddenly recognized as the strongest impulse of her being!

"Free! Body and soul free!" she kept whispering.

Josephine was kneeling before the closed door with her lips to the keyhole, imploring for admission. "Louise, open the door! I beg, open the door—you will make yourself ill. What are you doing, Louise? For heaven's sake open the door."

"Go away. I am not making myself ill." No; she was drinking in a very elixir of life through that open window.

Her fancy was running riot along those days ahead of her. Spring days, and summer days, and all sorts of days that would be her own. She breathed a quick prayer that life might be long. It was only yesterday she had thought with a shudder that life might be long.

She arose at length and opened the door to her sister's importunities. There was a feverish triumph in her eyes, and she carried herself unwittingly like a goddess of Victory. She clasped her sister's waist, and together they descended the stairs. Richards stood waiting for them at the bottom.

Someone was opening the front door with a latchkey. It was Brently Mallard who entered, a little travel-stained, composedly carrying his grip-sack and umbrella. He had been far from the scene of the accident, and did not even know there had been one.

He stood amazed at Josephine's piercing cry; at Richards' quick motion to screen him from the view of his wife.

But Richards was too late.

When the doctors came they said she had died of heart disease— of the joy that kills.

THE RECKONING[1]

Edith Wharton

"THE MARRIAGE LAW of the new dispensation will be: *Thou shalt not be unfaithful—to thyself.*"

A discreet murmur of approval filled the studio, and through the haze of cigarette smoke Mrs. Clement Westall, as her husband descended from his improvised platform, saw him merged in a congratulatory group of ladies. Westall's informal talks on "The New Ethics" had drawn about him an eager following of the mentally unemployed—those who, as he had once phrased it, liked to have their brain-food cut up for them. The talks had begun by accident. Westall's ideas were known to be "advanced," but hitherto their advance had not been in the direction of publicity. He had been, in his wife's opinion, almost pusillanimously careful not to let his personal views endanger his professional standing. Of late, however, he had shown a puzzling tendency to dogmatize, to throw down the gauntlet, to flaunt his private code in the face of society; and the relation of the sexes being a topic always sure of an audience, a few admiring friends had persuaded him to give his after-dinner opinions a larger circulation by summing them up in a series of talks at the Van Sideren studio.

The Herbert Van Siderens were a couple who subsisted, socially, on the fact that they had a studio. Van Sideren's pictures were chiefly valuable as accessories to the *mise en scene* which differentiated

1   First published in *Harper's Magazine* 105 (June 1, 1902: 145–160); reprinted in Wharton, *The Descent of Man* (New York: Scribner's 1904). This version corresponds to the one published in *The Descent of Man*; spelling has been adjusted to reflect current American usage.

his wife's "afternoons" from the blighting functions held in long New York drawing-rooms, and permitted her to offer their friends whiskey-and-soda instead of tea. Mrs. Van Sideren, for her part, was skilled in making the most of the kind of atmosphere which a lay-figure and an easel create; and if at times she found the illusion hard to maintain, and lost courage to the extent of almost wishing that Herbert could paint, she promptly overcame such moments of weakness by calling in some fresh talent, some extraneous re-en-forcement of the "artistic" impression. It was in quest of such aid that she had seized on Westall, coaxing him, somewhat to his wife's surprise, into a flattered participation in her fraud. It was vaguely felt, in the Van Sideren circle, that all the audacities were artistic, and that a teacher who pronounced marriage immoral was some-how as distinguished as a painter who depicted purple grass and a green sky. The Van Sideren set were tired of the conventional col-or-scheme in art and conduct.

Julia Westall had long had her own views on the immorality of marriage; she might indeed have claimed her husband as a disciple. In the early days of their union she had secretly resented his disin-clination to proclaim himself a follower of the new creed; had been inclined to tax him with moral cowardice, with a failure to live up to the convictions for which their marriage was supposed to stand. That was in the first burst of propagandism, when, womanlike, she wanted to turn her disobedience into a law. Now she felt differently. She could hardly account for the change, yet being a woman who never allowed her impulses to remain unaccounted for, she tried to do so by saying that she did not care to have the articles of her faith misinterpreted by the vulgar. In this connection, she was beginning to think that almost every one was vulgar; certainly there were few to whom she would have cared to entrust the defense of so esoteric a doctrine. And it was precisely at this point that Westall, discarding his unspoken principles, had chosen to descend from the heights of privacy, and stand hawking his convictions at the street-corner!

It was Una Van Sideren who, on this occasion, unconsciously focussed upon herself Mrs. Westall's wandering resentment. In the first place, the girl had no business to be there. It was "horrid"—Mrs. Westall found herself slipping back into the old feminine vocabulary—simply "horrid" to think of a young girl's being allowed to listen to such talk. The fact that Una smoked cigarettes and sipped an occasional cocktail did not in the least tarnish a certain radiant innocency which made her appear the victim, rather than the accomplice, of her parents' vulgarities. Julia Westall felt in a hot helpless way that something ought to be done—that someone ought to speak to the girl's mother. And just then Una glided up.

"Oh, Mrs. Westall, how beautiful it was!" Una fixed her with large limpid eyes. "You believe it all, I suppose?" she asked with seraphic gravity.

"All—what, my dear child?"

The girl shone on her. "About the higher life—the freer expansion of the individual—the law of fidelity to one's self," she glibly recited.

Mrs. Westall, to her own wonder, blushed a deep and burning blush.

"My dear Una," she said, "you don't in the least understand what it's all about!"

Miss Van Sideren stared, with a slowly answering blush. "Don't *you*, then?" she murmured.

Mrs. Westall laughed. "Not always—or altogether! But I should like some tea, please."

Una led her to the corner where innocent beverages were dispensed. As Julia received her cup she scrutinised the girl more carefully. It was not such a girlish face, after all—definite lines were forming under the rosy haze of youth. She reflected that Una must be six-and-twenty, and wondered why she had not married. A nice stock of ideas she would have as her dower! If *they* were to be a part of the modern girl's trousseau—

Mrs. Westall caught herself up with a start. It was as though someone else had been speaking—a stranger who had borrowed her own voice: she felt herself the dupe of some fantastic mental ventriloquism. Concluding suddenly that the room was stifling and Una's tea too sweet, she set down her cup, and looked about for Westall: to meet his eyes had long been her refuge from every uncertainty. She met them now, but only, as she felt, in transit; they included her parenthetically in a larger flight. She followed the flight, and it carried her to a corner to which Una had withdrawn—one of the palmy nooks to which Mrs. Van Sideren attributed the success of her Saturdays. Westall, a moment later, had overtaken his look, and found a place at the girl's side. She bent forward, speaking eagerly; he leaned back, listening, with the depreciatory smile which acted as a filter to flattery, enabling him to swallow the strongest doses without apparent grossness of appetite. Julia winced at her own definition of the smile.

On the way home, in the deserted winter dusk, Westall surprised his wife by a sudden boyish pressure of her arm. "Did I open their eyes a bit? Did I tell them what you wanted me to?" he asked gaily.

Almost unconsciously, she let her arm slip from his. "What *I* wanted—?"

"Why, haven't you—all this time?" She caught the honest wonder of his tone. "I somehow fancied you'd rather blamed me for not talking more openly—before—. You almost made me feel, at times, that I was sacrificing principles to expediency."

She paused a moment over her reply; then she asked quietly: "What made you decide not to—any longer?"

She felt again the vibration of a faint surprise. "Why—the wish to please you!" he answered, almost too simply.

"I wish you would not go on, then," she said abruptly.

He stopped in his quick walk, and she felt his stare through the darkness.

"Not go on—?"

"Call a hansom, please. I'm tired," broke from her with a sudden rush of physical weariness.

Instantly his solicitude enveloped her. The room had been infernally hot—and then that confounded cigarette smoke—he had noticed once or twice that she looked pale—she mustn't come to another Saturday. She felt herself yielding, as she always did, to the warm influence of his concern for her, the feminine in her leaning on the man in him with a conscious intensity of abandonment. He put her in the hansom, and her hand stole into his in the darkness. A tear or two rose, and she let them fall. It was so delicious to cry over imaginary troubles!

That evening, after dinner, he surprised her by reverting to the subject of his talk. He combined a man's dislike of uncomfortable questions with an almost feminine skill in eluding them; and she knew that if he returned to the subject he must have some special reason for doing so.

"You seem not to have cared for what I said this afternoon. Did I put the case badly?"

"No—you put it very well."

"Then what did you mean by saying that you would rather not have me go on with it?"

She glanced at him nervously, her ignorance of his intention deepening her sense of helplessness.

"I don't think I care to hear such things discussed in public."

"I don't understand you," he exclaimed. Again the feeling that his surprise was genuine gave an air of obliquity to her own attitude. She was not sure that she understood herself.

"Won't you explain?" he said with a tinge of impatience.

Her eyes wandered about the familiar drawing-room which had been the scene of so many of their evening confidences. The shaded lamps, the quiet-colored walls hung with mezzotints, the pale spring flowers scattered here and there in Venice glasses and bowls of old Sevres, recalled, she hardly knew why, the apartment in which the evenings of her first marriage had been passed—a wilderness of rosewood and upholstery, with a picture of a Roman peasant above the mantel-piece, and a Greek slave in "statuary marble" between the folding-doors of the back drawing-room. It was a room with which she had never been able to establish any closer relation than that between a traveler and a railway station; and now, as she looked about at the surroundings which stood for her deepest affinities— the room for which she had left that other room—she was startled by the same sense of strangeness and unfamiliarity. The prints, the flowers, the subdued tones of the old porcelains, seemed to typify a superficial refinement that had no relation to the deeper significances of life.

Suddenly she heard her husband repeating his question.

"I don't know that I can explain," she faltered.

He drew his arm-chair forward so that he faced her across the hearth. The light of a reading-lamp fell on his finely drawn face, which had a kind of surface-sensitiveness akin to the surface-refinement of its setting.

"Is it that you no longer believe in our ideas?" he asked.

"In our ideas—?"

"The ideas I am trying to teach. The ideas you and I are supposed to stand for." He paused a moment. "The ideas on which our marriage was founded."

The blood rushed to her face. He had his reasons, then—she was sure now that he had his reasons! In the ten years of their marriage, how often had either of them stopped to consider the ideas on which it was founded? How often does a man dig about the basement of his house to examine its foundation? The foundation is there, of course—the house rests on it—but one lives abovestairs and not in the cellar. It was she, indeed, who in the beginning had insisted on reviewing the situation now and then, on recapitulating the reasons which justified her course, on proclaiming, from time to time, her adherence to the religion of personal independence;

but she had long ceased to feel the need of any such ideal standards, and had accepted her marriage as frankly and naturally as though it had been based on the primitive needs of the heart, and needed no special sanction to explain or justify it.

"Of course I still believe in our ideas!" she exclaimed.

"Then I repeat that I don't understand. It was a part of your theory that the greatest possible publicity should be given to our view of marriage. Have you changed your mind in that respect?"

She hesitated. "It depends on circumstances—on the public one is addressing. The set of people that the Van Siderens get about them don't care for the truth or falseness of a doctrine. They are attracted simply by its novelty."

"And yet it was in just such a set of people that you and I met, and learned the truth from each other."

"That was different."

"In what way?"

"I was not a young girl, to begin with. It is perfectly unfitting that young girls should be present at—at such times—should hear such things discussed—"

"I thought you considered it one of the deepest social wrongs that such things never *are* discussed before young girls; but that is beside the point, for I don't remember seeing any young girl in my audience to-day—"

"Except Una Van Sideren!"

He turned slightly and pushed back the lamp at his elbow.

"Oh, Miss Van Sideren—naturally—"

"Why naturally?"

"The daughter of the house—would you have had her sent out with her governess?"

"If I had a daughter I should not allow such things to go on in my house!"

Westall, stroking his mustache, leaned back with a faint smile. "I fancy Miss Van Sideren is quite capable of taking care of herself."

"No girl knows how to take care of herself—till it's too late."

"And yet you would deliberately deny her the surest means of self-defense?"

"What do you call the surest means of self-defense?"

"Some preliminary knowledge of human nature in its relation to the marriage tie."

She made an impatient gesture. "How should you like to marry that kind of a girl?"

"Immensely—if she were my kind of girl in other respects."

She took up the argument at another point.

"You are quite mistaken if you think such talk does not affect young girls. Una was in a state of the most absurd exaltation—" She broke off, wondering why she had spoken.

Westall reopened a magazine which he had laid aside at the beginning of their discussion. "What you tell me is immensely flattering to my oratorical talent—but I fear you overrate its effect. I can assure you that Miss Van Sideren doesn't have to have her thinking done for her. She's quite capable of doing it herself."

"You seem very familiar with her mental processes!" flashed unguardedly from his wife.

He looked up quietly from the pages he was cutting.

"I should like to be," he answered. "She interests me."

II

If there be a distinction in being misunderstood, it was one denied to Julia Westall when she left her first husband. Everyone was ready to excuse and even to defend her. The world she adorned agreed that John Arment was "impossible," and hostesses gave a sigh of relief at the thought that it would no longer be necessary to ask him to dine.

There had been no scandal connected with the divorce: neither side had accused the other of the offence euphemistically described as "statutory." The Arments had indeed been obliged to transfer their allegiance to a State which recognized desertion as a cause for divorce, and construed the term so liberally that the seeds of desertion were shown to exist in every union. Even Mrs. Arment's second marriage did not make traditional morality stir in its sleep. It was known that she had not met her second husband till after she had parted from the first, and she had, moreover, replaced a rich man by a poor one. Though Clement Westall was acknowledged to be a rising lawyer, it was generally felt that his fortunes would not rise as rapidly as his reputation. The Westalls would probably always have to live quietly and go out to dinner in cabs. Could there be better evidence of Mrs. Arment's complete disinterestedness?

If the reasoning by which her friends justified her course was somewhat cruder and less complex than her own elucidation of the matter, both explanations led to the same conclusion: John Arment was impossible. The only difference was that, to his wife, his impossibility was something deeper than a social disqualification. She had once said, in ironical defense of her marriage, that it had at least preserved her from the necessity of sitting next to him at dinner; but she had not then realized at what cost the immunity was purchased. John Arment was impossible; but the sting of his impossibility lay in the fact that he made it impossible for those about him to be other than himself. By an unconscious process of elimination he had excluded from the world everything of which he did not feel a personal need: had become, as it were, a climate in which only his own requirements survived. This might seem to imply a deliberate selfishness; but there was nothing deliberate about Arment. He was as instinctive as an animal or a child. It was this childish element in his nature which sometimes for a moment unsettled his wife's estimate of him. Was it possible that he was simply undeveloped, that he had delayed, somewhat longer than is usual, the laborious process of growing up? He had the kind of sporadic shrewdness which causes it to be said of a dull man that he is "no fool"; and it was this quality that his wife found most trying. Even to the naturalist it is annoying to have his deductions disturbed by some unforeseen aberrancy of form or function; and how much more so to the wife whose estimate of herself is inevitably bound up with her judgment of her husband!

Arment's shrewdness did not, indeed, imply any latent intellectual power; it suggested, rather, potentialities of feeling, of suffering, perhaps, in a blind rudimentary way, on which Julia's sensibilities naturally declined to linger. She so fully understood her own reasons for leaving him that she disliked to think they were not as comprehensible to her husband. She was haunted, in her analytic moments, by the look of perplexity, too inarticulate for words, with which he had acquiesced to her explanations.

These moments were rare with her, however. Her marriage had been too concrete a misery to be surveyed philosophically. If she had been unhappy for complex reasons, the unhappiness was as real as though it had been uncomplicated. Soul is more bruisable than flesh, and Julia was wounded in every fiber of her spirit. Her husband's personality seemed to be closing gradually in on her, obscuring the sky and cutting off the air, till she felt herself shut up among the decaying bodies of her starved hopes. A sense of having been decoyed by some world-old conspiracy into this bondage of body and soul filled her with despair. If marriage was the slow lifelong acquittal of a debt contracted in ignorance, then marriage was a crime against human nature. She, for one, would have no share in maintaining the pretense of which she had been a victim: the pretense that a man and a woman, forced into the narrowest of personal relations, must remain there till the end, though they may have outgrown the span of each other's natures as the mature tree outgrows the iron brace about the sapling.

It was in the first heat of her moral indignation that she had met Clement Westall. She had seen at once that he was "interested," and had fought off the discovery, dreading any influence that should draw her back into the bondage of conventional relations. To ward off the peril she had, with an almost crude precipitancy, revealed her opinions to him. To her surprise, she found that he shared them. She was attracted by the frankness of a suitor who, while pressing his suit, admitted that he did not believe in marriage. Her worst audacities did not seem to surprise him: he had thought out all that she had felt, and they had reached the same conclusion. People grew at varying rates, and the yoke that was an easy fit for the one might soon become galling to the other. That was what divorce was for: the readjustment of personal relations. As soon as their necessarily transitive nature was recognized they would gain in dignity as well as in harmony. There would be no farther need of the ignoble concessions and connivances, the perpetual sacrifice of personal delicacy and moral pride, by means of which imperfect marriages were now held together. Each partner to the contract would be on his mettle, forced to live up to the highest standard of self-development, on pain of losing the other's respect and affection. The low nature could no longer drag the higher down, but must struggle to rise, or remain alone on its inferior level. The only necessary condition to a harmonious marriage was a frank recognition of this truth, and a solemn agreement between the contracting parties to keep faith with themselves, and not to live together for a moment after complete accord had ceased to exist between them. The new adultery was unfaithfulness to self.

It was, as Westall had just reminded her, on this understanding that they had married. The ceremony was an unimportant concession to social prejudice: now that the door of divorce stood open, no marriage need be an imprisonment, and the contract therefore no longer involved any diminution of self-respect. The nature of their attachment placed them so far beyond the reach of such contingencies that it was easy to discuss them with an open mind; and Julia's sense of security made her dwell with a tender insistence on Westall's promise to claim his release when he should cease to love her. The exchange of these vows seemed to make them, in a sense, champions of the new law, pioneers in the forbidden realm of individual freedom: they felt that they had somehow achieved beatitude without martyrdom.

This, as Julia now reviewed the past, she perceived to have been her theoretical attitude toward marriage. It was unconsciously, insidiously, that her ten years of happiness with Westall had developed another conception of the tie; a reversion, rather, to the old instinct of passionate dependency and possessorship that now made her blood revolt at the mere hint of change. Change? Renewal? Was that what they had called it, in their foolish jargon? Destruction, extermination rather—this rending of a myriad fibers interwoven with another's being! Another? But he was not other! He and she were one, one in the mystic sense which alone gave marriage its significance. The new law was not for them, but for the disunited creatures forced into a mockery of union. The gospel she had felt called on to proclaim had no bearing on her own case.... She sent for the doctor and told him she was sure she needed a nerve tonic.

She took the nerve tonic diligently, but it failed to act as a sedative to her fears. She did not know what she feared; but that made her anxiety the more pervasive. Her husband had not reverted to the subject of his Saturday talks. He was unusually kind and considerate, with a softening of his quick manner, a touch of shyness in his consideration, that sickened her with new fears. She told herself that it was because she looked badly—because he knew about the doctor and the nerve tonic—that he showed this deference to her wishes, this eagerness to screen her from moral draughts; but the explanation simply cleared the way for fresh inferences.

The week passed slowly, vacantly, like a prolonged Sunday. On Saturday the morning post brought a note from Mrs. Van Sideren. Would dear Julia ask Mr. Westall to come half an hour earlier than usual, as there was to be some music after his "talk"? Westall was just leaving for his office when his wife read the note. She opened the drawing-room door and called him back to deliver the message.

He glanced at the note and tossed it aside. "What a bore! I shall have to cut my game of racquets. Well, I suppose it can't be helped. Will you write and say it's all right?"

Julia hesitated a moment, her hand stiffening on the chair-back against which she leaned.

"You mean to go on with these talks?" she asked.

"I—why not?" he returned; and this time it struck her that his surprise was not quite unfeigned. The discovery helped her to find words.

"You said you had started them with the idea of pleasing me—"
"Well?"

"I told you last week that they didn't please me."

"Last week? Oh—" He seemed to make an effort of memory. "I thought you were nervous then; you sent for the doctor the next day."

"It was not the doctor I needed; it was your assurance—"
"My assurance?"

Suddenly she felt the floor fail under her. She sank into the chair with a choking throat, her words, her reasons slipping away from her like straws down a whirling flood.

"Clement," she cried, "isn't it enough for you to know that I hate it?"

He turned to close the door behind them; then he walked toward her and sat down. "What is it that you hate?" he asked gently.

She had made a desperate effort to rally her routed argument.

"I can't bear to have you speak as if—as if—our marriage—were like the other kind—the wrong kind. When I heard you there, the other afternoon, before all those inquisitive gossiping people, pro-claiming that husbands and wives had a right to leave each other whenever they were tired—or had seen someone else—"

Westall sat motionless, his eyes fixed on a pattern of the carpet.

"You *have* ceased to take this view, then?" he said as she broke off. "You no longer believe that husbands and wives *are* justified in separating—under such conditions?"

"Under such conditions?" she stammered. "Yes—I still believe that—but how can we judge for others? What can we know of the circumstances—?"

He interrupted her. "I thought it was a fundamental article of our creed that the special circumstances produced by marriage were not to interfere with the full assertion of individual liberty." He paused a moment. "I thought that was your reason for leaving Arment."

She flushed to the forehead. It was not like him to give a personal turn to the argument.

"It was my reason," she said simply.

"Well, then—why do you refuse to recognize its validity now?"

"I don't—I don't—I only say that one can't judge for others."

He made an impatient movement. "This is mere hair-splitting. What you mean is that, the doctrine having served your purpose when you needed it, you now repudiate it."

"Well," she exclaimed, flushing again, "what if I do? What does it matter to us?"

Westall rose from his chair. He was excessively pale, and stood before his wife with something of the formality of a stranger.

"It matters to me," he said in a low voice, "because I do *not* repudiate it."

"Well—?"

"And because I had intended to invoke it as—"

He paused and drew his breath deeply. She sat silent, almost deafened by her heart-beats.

"—as a complete justification of the course I am about to take."

Julia remained motionless. "What course is that?" she asked.

He cleared his throat. "I mean to claim the fulfilment of your promise."

For an instant the room wavered and darkened; then she recovered a torturing acuteness of vision. Every detail of her surroundings pressed upon her: the tick of the clock, the slant of sunlight on the wall, the hardness of the chair-arms that she grasped, were a separate wound to each sense.

"My promise—" she faltered.

"Your part of our mutual agreement to set each other free if one or the other should wish to be released."

She was silent again. He waited a moment, shifting his position nervously; then he said, with a touch of irritability: "You acknowledge the agreement?"

The question went through her like a shock. She lifted her head to it proudly. "I acknowledge the agreement," she said.

"And—you don't mean to repudiate it?"

A log on the hearth fell forward, and mechanically he advanced and pushed it back.

"No," she answered slowly, "I don't mean to repudiate it."

There was a pause. He remained near the hearth, his elbow resting on the mantel-shelf. Close to his hand stood a little cup of jade that he had given her on one of their wedding anniversaries. She wondered vaguely if he noticed it.

"You intend to leave me, then?" she said at length.

His gesture seemed to deprecate the crudeness of the allusion.

"To marry some one else?"

Again his eye and hand protested. She rose and stood before him.

"Why should you be afraid to tell me? Is it Una Van Sideren?"

He was silent.

"I wish you good luck," she said.

III

She looked up, finding herself alone. She did not remember when or how he had left the room, or how long afterward she had sat there. The fire still smoldered on the hearth, but the slant of sunlight had left the wall.

Her first conscious thought was that she had not broken her
word, that she had fulfilled the very letter of their bargain. There
had been no crying out, no vain appeal to the past, no attempt at
temporizing or evasion. She had marched straight up to the guns.

Now that it was over, she sickened to find herself alive. She looked
about her, trying to recover her hold on reality. Her identity seemed
to be slipping from her, as it disappears in a physical swoon. "This
is my room—this is my house," she heard herself saying. Her room?
Her house? She could almost hear the walls laugh back at her.

She stood up, a dull ache in every bone. The silence of the room
frightened her. She remembered, now, having heard the front door
close a long time ago: the sound suddenly re-echoed through her
brain. Her husband must have left the house, then—her *husband?*
She no longer knew in what terms to think: the simplest phrases
had a poisoned edge. She sank back into her chair, overcome by
a strange weakness. The clock struck ten—it was only ten o'clock!
Suddenly she remembered that she had not ordered dinner...or were
they dining out that evening? *Dinner—dining out*—the old meaningless phraseology pursued her! She must try to think of herself
as she would think of someone else, a someone dissociated from
all the familiar routine of the past, whose wants and habits must
gradually be learned, as one might spy out the ways of a strange
animal....

The clock struck another hour—eleven. She stood up again
and walked to the door: she thought she would go upstairs to her
room. *Her* room? Again the word derided her. She opened the door,
crossed the narrow hall, and walked up the stairs. As she passed,
she noticed Westall's sticks and umbrellas: a pair of his gloves lay
on the hall table. The same stair-carpet mounted between the same
walls; the same old French print, in its narrow black frame, faced
her on the landing. This visual continuity was intolerable. Within,
a gaping chasm; without, the same untroubled and familiar surface.
She must get away from it before she could attempt to think. But,

once in her room, she sat down on the lounge, a stupor creeping over her....

Gradually her vision cleared. A great deal had happened in the interval—a wild marching and countermarching of emotions, arguments, ideas—a fury of insurgent impulses that fell back spent upon themselves. She had tried, at first, to rally, to organize these chaotic forces. There must be help somewhere, if only she could master the inner tumult. Life could not be broken off short like this, for a whim, a fancy; the law itself would side with her, would defend her. The law? What claim had she upon it? She was the prisoner of her own choice: she had been her own legislator, and she was the predestined victim of the code she had devised. But this was grotesque, intolerable—a mad mistake, for which she could not be held accountable! The law she had despised was still there, might still be invoked...invoked, but to what end? Could she ask it to chain Westall to her side? *She* had been allowed to go free when she claimed her freedom—should she show less magnanimity than she had exacted? Magnanimity? The word lashed her with its irony— one does not strike an attitude when one is fighting for life! She would threaten, grovel, cajole...she would yield anything to keep her hold on happiness. Ah, but the difficulty lay deeper! The law could not help her—her own apostasy could not help her. She was the victim of the theories she renounced. It was as though some giant machine of her own making had caught her up in its wheels and was grinding her to atoms....

It was afternoon when she found herself out-of-doors. She walked with an aimless haste, fearing to meet familiar faces. The day was radiant, metallic: one of those searching American days so calculated to reveal the shortcomings of our street-cleaning and the excesses of our architecture. The streets looked bare and hideous; everything stared and glittered. She called a passing hansom, and gave Mrs. Van Sideren's address. She did not know what had led up to the act; but she found herself suddenly resolved to speak, to cry out a warning. It was too late to save herself—but the girl might still be told. The hansom rattled up Fifth Avenue; she sat with her eyes fixed, avoiding recognition. At the Van Siderens' door she sprang out and rang the bell. Action had cleared her brain, and she felt calm and self-possessed. She knew now exactly what she meant to say.

The ladies were both out…the parlor-maid stood waiting for a card. Julia, with a vague murmur, turned away from the door and lingered a moment on the sidewalk. Then she remembered that she had not paid the cab-driver. She drew a dollar from her purse and handed it to him. He touched his hat and drove off, leaving her alone in the long empty street. She wandered away westward, toward strange thoroughfares, where she was not likely to meet acquaintances. The feeling of aimlessness had returned. Once she found herself in the afternoon torrent of Broadway, swept past tawdry shops and flaming theatrical posters, with a succession of meaningless faces gliding by in the opposite direction….

A feeling of faintness reminded her that she had not eaten since morning. She turned into a side street of shabby houses, with rows of ash-barrels behind bent area railings. In a basement window she saw the sign *Ladies' Restaurant:* a pie and a dish of doughnuts lay against the dusty pane like petrified food in an ethnological museum. She entered, and a young woman with a weak mouth and a brazen eye cleared a table for her near the window. The table was covered with a red and white cotton cloth and adorned with a bunch of celery in a thick tumbler and a salt-cellar full of grayish lumpy salt. Julia ordered tea, and sat a long time waiting for it. She was glad to be away from the noise and confusion of the streets. The low-ceilinged room was empty, and two or three waitresses with thin pert faces lounged in the background staring at her and whispering together. At last the tea was brought in a discolored metal teapot. Julia poured a cup and drank it hastily. It was black and bitter, but it flowed through her veins like an elixir. She was almost dizzy with exhilaration. Oh, how tired, how unutterably tired she had been!

She drank a second cup, blacker and bitterer, and now her mind was once more working clearly. She felt as vigorous, as decisive, as when she had stood on the Van Siderens' door-step—but the wish to return there had subsided. She saw now the futility of such an attempt—the humiliation to which it might have exposed her....The pity of it was that she did not know what to do next. The short winter day was fading, and she realized that she could not remain much longer in the restaurant without attracting notice. She paid for her tea and went out into the street. The lamps were alight, and here and there a basement shop cast an oblong of gaslight across the fissured pavement. In the dusk there was something sinister about the aspect of the street, and she hastened back toward Fifth Avenue. She was not used to being out alone at that hour.

At the corner of Fifth Avenue she paused and stood watching the stream of carriages. At last a policeman caught sight of her and signed to her that he would take her across. She had not meant to cross the street, but she obeyed automatically, and presently found herself on the farther corner. There she paused again for a moment; but she fancied the policeman was watching her, and this sent her hastening down the nearest side street....After that she walked a long time, vaguely.... Night had fallen, and now and then, through the windows of a passing carriage, she caught the expanse of an evening waistcoat or the shimmer of an opera cloak....

Suddenly she found herself in a familiar street. She stood still a moment, breathing quickly. She had turned the corner without noticing whither it led; but now, a few yards ahead of her, she saw the house in which she had once lived—her first husband's house. The blinds were drawn, and only a faint translucence marked the windows and the transom above the door. As she stood there she heard a step behind her, and a man walked by in the direction of the house. He walked slowly, with a heavy middle-aged gait, his head sunk a little between the shoulders, the red crease of his neck visible above the fur collar of his overcoat. He crossed the street, went up the steps of the house, drew forth a latch-key, and let himself in...

There was no one else in sight. Julia leaned for a long time against the area-rail at the corner, her eyes fixed on the front of the house. The feeling of physical weariness had returned, but the strong tea still throbbed in her veins and lit her brain with an unnatural clearness. Presently she heard another step draw near, and moving quickly away, she too crossed the street and mounted the steps of the house. The impulse which had carried her there prolonged itself in a quick pressure of the electric bell—then she felt suddenly weak and tremulous, and grasped the balustrade for support. The door opened and a young footman with a fresh inexperienced face stood on the threshold. Julia knew in an instant that he would admit her.

"I saw Mr. Arment going in just now," she said. "Will you ask him to see me for a moment?"

The footman hesitated. "I think Mr. Arment has gone up to dress for dinner, madam."

Julia advanced into the hall. "I am sure he will see me—I will not detain him long," she said. She spoke quietly, authoritatively, in the tone which a good servant does not mistake. The footman had his hand on the drawing-room door.

"I will tell him, madam. What name, please?"

Julia trembled: she had not thought of that. "Merely say a lady," she returned carelessly.

The footman wavered and she fancied herself lost; but at that instant the door opened from within and John Arment stepped into the hall. He drew back sharply as he saw her, his florid face turning sallow with the shock; then the blood poured back to it, swelling the veins on his temples and reddening the lobes of his thick ears.

It was long since Julia had seen him, and she was startled at the change in his appearance. He had thickened, coarsened, settled down into the enclosing flesh. But she noted this insensibly: her one conscious thought was that, now she was face to face with him, she must not let him escape till he had heard her. Every pulse in her body throbbed with the urgency of her message.

She went up to him as he drew back. "I must speak to you," she said.

Arment hesitated, red and stammering. Julia glanced at the footman, and her look acted as a warning. The instinctive shrinking from a "scene" predominated over every other impulse, and Arment said slowly: "Will you come this way?"

He followed her into the drawing-room and closed the door. Julia, as she advanced, was vaguely aware that the room at least was unchanged: time had not mitigated its horrors. The contadina still lurched from the chimney-breast, and the Greek slave obstructed the threshold of the inner room. The place was alive with memories: they started out from every fold of the yellow satin curtains and glided between the angles of the rosewood furniture. But while some subordinate agency was carrying these impressions to her brain, her whole conscious effort was centered in the act of dominating Arment's will. The fear that he would refuse to hear her mounted like fever to her brain. She felt her purpose melt before it, words and arguments running into each other in the heat of her longing. For a moment her voice failed her, and she imagined herself thrust out before she could speak; but as she was struggling for a word, Arment pushed a chair forward, and said quietly: "You are not well."

The sound of his voice steadied her. It was neither kind nor unkind—a voice that suspended judgment, rather, awaiting unforeseen developments. She supported herself against the back of the chair and drew a deep breath. "Shall I send for something?" he continued, with a cold embarrassed politeness.

Julia raised an entreating hand. "No—no—thank you. I am quite well."

He paused midway toward the bell and turned on her. "Then may I ask—?"

"Yes," she interrupted him. "I came here because I wanted to see you. There is something I must tell you."

Arment continued to scrutinize her. "I am surprised at that," he said. "I should have supposed that any communication you may wish to make could have been made through our lawyers."

"Our lawyers!" She burst into a little laugh. "I don't think they could help me—this time."

Arment's face took on a barricaded look. "If there is any question of help—of course—"

It struck her, whimsically, that she had seen that look when some shabby devil called with a subscription-book. Perhaps he thought she wanted him to put his name down for so much in sympathy—or even in money....The thought made her laugh again. She saw his look change slowly to perplexity. All his facial changes were slow, and she remembered, suddenly, how it had once diverted her to shift that lumbering scenery with a word. For the first time it struck her that she had been cruel. "There *is* a question of help," she said in a softer key: "you can help me; but only by listening.... I want to tell you something...."

Arment's resistance was not yielding. "Would it not be easier to—write?" he suggested.

She shook her head. "There is no time to write...and it won't take long." She raised her head and their eyes met. "My husband has left me," she said.

"Westall—?" he stammered, reddening again.

"Yes. This morning. Just as I left you. Because he was tired of me."

The words, uttered scarcely above a whisper, seemed to dilate to the limit of the room. Arment looked toward the door; then his embarrassed glance returned to Julia.

"I am very sorry," he said awkwardly.

"Thank you," she murmured.

"But I don't see—"

"No—but you will—in a moment. Won't you listen to me? Please!" Instinctively she had shifted her position putting herself between him and the door. "It happened this morning," she went on in short breathless phrases. "I never suspected anything—I thought we were—perfectly happy.... Suddenly he told me he was tired of me...there is a girl he likes better...He has gone to her...." As she spoke, the lurking anguish rose upon her, possessing her once more to the exclusion of every other emotion. Her eyes ached, her throat swelled with it, and two painful tears ran down her face.

Arment's constraint was increasing visibly. "This—this is very unfortunate," he began. "But I should say the law—"

"The law?" she echoed ironically. "When he asks for his freedom?"

"You are not obliged to give it."

"You were not obliged to give me mine—but you did."

He made a protesting gesture.

"You saw that the law couldn't help you—didn't you?" she went on. "That is what I see now. The law represents material rights—it can't go beyond. If we don't recognize an inner law....the obligation that love creates....being loved as well as loving....there is nothing to prevent our spreading ruin unhindered....is there?" She raised her head plaintively, with the look of a bewildered child. "That is what I see now....what I wanted to tell you. He leaves me because he's tired....but *I* was not tired; and I don't understand why he is. That's the dreadful part of it—the not understanding: I hadn't realized what it meant. But I've been thinking of it all day, and things have come back to me—things I hadn't noticed....when you and I...." She moved closer to him, and fixed her eyes on his with the gaze that tries to reach beyond words. "I see now that *you* didn't understand—did you?"

Their eyes met in a sudden shock of comprehension: a veil seemed to be lifted between them. Arment's lip trembled.

"No," he said, "I didn't understand."

She gave a little cry, almost of triumph. "I knew it! I knew it! You wondered—you tried to tell me—but no words came.... You saw your life falling in ruins…the world slipping from you…and you couldn't speak or move!"

She sank down on the chair against which she had been leaning. "Now I know—now I know," she repeated.

"I am very sorry for you," she heard Arment stammer.

She looked up quickly. "That's not what I came for. I don't want you to be sorry. I came to ask you to forgive me…for not understanding that *you* didn't understand….That's all I wanted to say." She rose with a vague sense that the end had come, and put out a groping hand toward the door.

Arment stood motionless. She turned to him with a faint smile.

"You forgive me?"

"There is nothing to forgive—"

"Then will you shake hands for good-by?" She felt his hand in hers: it was nerveless, reluctant.

"Good-by," she repeated. "I understand now."

She opened the door and passed out into the hall. As she did so, Arment took an impulsive step forward; but just then the footman, who was evidently alive to his obligations, advanced from the background to let her out. She heard Arment fall back. The footman threw open the door, and she found herself outside in the darkness.

MRS. SPRING FRAGRANCE[1]

Sui Sin Far

WHEN MRS. SPRING Fragrance first arrived in Seattle, she was unacquainted with even one word of the American language. Five years later her husband, speaking of her, said: "There are no more American words for her learning." And everyone who knew Mrs. Spring Fragrance agreed with Mr. Spring Fragrance.

Mr. Spring Fragrance, whose business name was Sing Yook, was a young curio merchant. Though conservatively Chinese in many respects, he was at the same time what is called by the Westerners, "Americanized." Mrs. Spring Fragrance was even more "Americanized."

Next door to the Spring Fragrances lived the Chin Yuens. Mrs. Chin Yuen was much older than Mrs. Spring Fragrance; but she had a daughter of eighteen with whom Mrs. Spring Fragrance was on terms of great friendship. The daughter was a pretty girl whose Chinese name was Mai Gwi Far (a rose) and whose American name was Laura. Nearly everybody called her Laura, even her parents and Chinese friends. Laura had a sweetheart, a youth named Kai Tzu. Kai Tzu, who was American-born, and as ruddy and stalwart as any young Westerner, was noted amongst baseball players as one of the finest pitchers on the Coast. He could also sing, "Drink to me only with thine eyes," to Laura's piano accompaniment.

Now the only person who knew that Kai Tzu loved Laura and that Laura loved Kai Tzu, was Mrs. Spring Fragrance. The reason for this was that, although the Chin Yuen parents lived in a house

---

1   First published in *Hampton's Magazine*, January 1910.

furnished in American style, and wore American clothes, yet they religiously observed many Chinese customs, and their ideals of life were the ideals of their Chinese forefathers. Therefore, they had betrothed their daughter, Laura, at the age of fifteen, to the eldest son of the Chinese Government school-teacher in San Francisco. The time for the consummation of the betrothal was approaching.

Laura was with Mrs. Spring Fragrance and Mrs. Spring Fragrance was trying to cheer her.

"I had such a pretty walk today," said she. "I crossed the banks above the beach and came back by the long road. In the green grass the daffodils were blowing, in the cottage gardens the currant bushes were flowering, and in the air was the perfume of the wallflower. I wished, Laura, that you were with me." Laura burst into tears. "That is the walk," she sobbed, "Kai Tzu and I so love; but never, ah, never, can we take it together again."

"Now, Little Sister," comforted Mrs. Spring Fragrance, "you really must not grieve like that. Is there not a beautiful American poem written by a noble American named Tennyson, which says:

'Tis better to have loved and lost,
Than never to have loved at all?"

Mrs. Spring Fragrance was unaware that Mr. Spring Fragrance, having returned from the city, tired with the day's business, had thrown himself down on the bamboo settee on the veranda, and that although his eyes were engaged in scanning the pages of the *Chinese World*, his ears could not help receiving the words which were borne to him through the open window.

"'Tis better to have loved and lost,
Than never to have loved at all?"

repeated Mr. Spring Fragrance. Not wishing to hear more of the secret talk of women, he arose and sauntered around the veranda to the other side of the house. Two pigeons circled around his head.

He felt in his pocket, for a li-chi which he usually carried for their pecking. His fingers touched a little box. It contained a jadestone pendant, which Mrs. Spring Fragrance had particularly admired the last time she was down town. It was the fifth anniversary of Mr. and Mrs. Spring Fragrance's wedding day.

Mr. Spring Fragrance pressed the little box down into the depths of his pocket.

A young man came out of the back door of the house at Mr. Spring Fragrance's left. The Chin Yuen house was at his right.

"Good evening," said the young man. "Good evening," returned Mr. Spring Fragrance. He stepped down from his porch and went and leaned over the railing which separated this yard from the yard in which stood the young man.

"Will you please tell me," said Mr. Spring Fragrance, "the meaning of two lines of an American verse which I have heard?"

"Certainly," returned the young man with a genial smile. He was a star student at the University of Washington, and had not the slightest doubt that he could explain the meaning of all things in the universe.

"Well," said Mr. Spring Fragrance, "it is this:

'Tis better to have loved and lost,
Than never to have loved at all?"

"Ah!" responded the young man with an air of profound wisdom. "That, Mr. Spring Fragrance, means that it is a good thing to love anyway—even if we can't get what we love, or, as the poet tells us, lose what we love. Of course, one needs experience to feel the truth of this teaching."

The young man smiled pensively and reminiscently. More than a dozen young maidens "loved and lost" were passing before his mind's eye.

"The truth of the teaching!" echoed Mr. Spring Fragrance, a little testily. "There is no truth in it whatever. It is disobedient to reason.

Is it not better to have what you do not love than to love what you do not have?"

"That depends," answered the young man, "upon temperament."

"I thank you. Good evening," said Mr. Spring Fragrance. He turned away to muse upon the unwisdom of the American way of looking at things.

Meanwhile, inside the house, Laura was refusing to be comforted.

"Ah, no! no!" cried she. "If I had not gone to school with Kai Tzu, nor talked nor walked with him, nor played the accompaniments to his songs, then I might consider with complacency, or at least without horror, my approaching marriage with the son of Man You. But as it is—oh, as it is—!"

The girl rocked herself to and fro in heartfelt grief.

Mrs. Spring Fragrance knelt down beside her, and clasping her arms around her neck, cried in sympathy:

"Little Sister, oh, Little Sister! Dry your tears—do not despair. A moon has yet to pass before the marriage can take place. Who knows what the stars may have to say to one another during its passing? A little bird has whispered to me—"

For a long time Mrs. Spring Fragrance talked. For a long time Laura listened. When the girl arose to go, there was a bright light in her eyes.

II

Mrs. Spring Fragrance, in San Francisco, on a visit to her cousin, the wife of the herb doctor of Clay Street, was having a good time. She was invited everywhere that the wife of an honorable Chinese merchant could go. There was much to see and hear, including more than a dozen babies who had been born in the families of her friends since she last visited the city of the Golden Gate. Mrs. Spring Fragrance loved babies. She had had two herself, but both had been transplanted into the spirit land before the completion of even one moon. There were also many dinners and theatre-parties given in her honor. It was at one of the theatre-parties that Mrs. Spring Fragrance met Ah Oi, a young girl who had the reputation of being the prettiest Chinese girl in San Francisco, and the naughtiest. In spite of gossip, however, Mrs. Spring Fragrance took a great fancy to Ah Oi and invited her to a tête-à-tête picnic on the following day. This invitation Ah Oi joyfully accepted. She was a sort of bird girl and never felt so happy as when out in the park or woods.

On the day after the picnic Mrs. Spring Fragrance wrote to Laura Chin Yuen thus:

> MY PRECIOUS LAURA,—May the bamboo ever wave. Next week I accompany Ah Oi to the beauteous town of San José. There will we be met by the son of the Illustrious Teacher, and in a little Mission, presided over by a benevolent American priest, the little Ah Oi and the son of the Illustrious Teacher will be joined together in love and harmony—two pieces of music made to complete one another.
>
> The Son of the Illustrious Teacher, having been through an American Hall of Learning, is well able to provide for his orphan bride and fears not the displeasure of his parents, now that he is assured that your grief at his loss will not be inconsolable. He wishes me to waft to you and to Kai Tzu—and the little Ah Oi joins with him—ten thousand rainbow wishes for your happiness.
>
> My respects to your honorable parents, and to yourself, the heart of your loving friend,
>
> JADE SPRING FRAGRANCE

To Mr. Spring Fragrance, Mrs. Spring Fragrance also indited a letter:

> GREAT AND HONORED MAN,—Greeting from your

plum blossom,[2] who is desirous of hiding herself from
the sun of your presence for a week of seven days more.
My honorable cousin is preparing for the Fifth Moon
Festival, and wishes me to compound for the occasion
some American "fudge," for which delectable sweet,
made by my clumsy hands, you have sometimes shown
a slight prejudice. I am enjoying a most agreeable visit,
and American friends, as also our own, strive benev-
olently for the accomplishment of my pleasure. Mrs.
Samuel Smith, an American lady, known to my cousin,
asked for my accompaniment to a magniloquent lecture the other evening. The subject was "America, the
Protector of China!" It was most exhilarating, and the
effect of so much expression of benevolence leads me to
beg of you to forget to remember that the barber charges
you one dollar for a shave while he humbly submits to
the American man a bill of fifteen cents. And murmur
no more because your honored elder brother, on a visit
to this country, is detained under the roof-tree of this
great Government instead of under your own humble
roof. Console him with the reflection that he is protected
under the wing of the Eagle, the Emblem of Liberty.
What is the loss of ten hundred years or ten thousand
times ten dollars compared with the happiness of
knowing oneself so securely sheltered? All of this I have
learned from Mrs. Samuel Smith, who is as brilliant and
great of mind as one of your own superior sex.

For me it is sufficient to know that the Golden Gate
Park is most enchanting, and the seals on the rock at the
Cliff House extremely entertaining and amiable. There
is much feasting and merry-making under the lanterns

2   The plum blossom is the Chinese flower of virtue. It has been adopted by
the Japanese in the same way as they have adopted the Chinese national flower,
the chrysanthemum.

in honor of your Stupid Thorn.

I have purchased for your smoking a pipe with an amber mouth. It is said to be very sweet to the lips and to emit a cloud of smoke fit for the gods to inhale.

Awaiting, by the wonderful wire of the telegram message, your gracious permission to remain for the celebration of the Fifth Moon Festival and the making of American "fudge," I continue for ten thousand times ten thousand years,

Your ever loving and obedient woman,

JADE

P.S. Forget not to care for the cat, the birds, and the flowers. Do not eat too quickly nor fan too vigorously now that the weather is warming.

Mrs. Spring Fragrance smiled as she folded this last epistle. Even if he were old-fashioned, there was never a husband so good and kind as hers. Only on one occasion since their marriage had he slighted her wishes. That was when, on the last anniversary of their wedding, she had signified a desire for a certain jadestone pendant, and he had failed to satisfy that desire.

But Mrs. Spring Fragrance, being of a happy nature, and disposed to look upon the bright side of things, did not allow her mind to dwell upon the jadestone pendant. Instead, she gazed complacently down upon her bejeweled fingers and folded in with her letter to Mr. Spring Fragrance a bright little sheaf of condensed love.

III

Mr. Spring Fragrance sat on his doorstep. He had been reading two letters, one from Mrs. Spring Fragrance, and the other from an elderly bachelor cousin in San Francisco. The one from the elderly bachelor cousin was a business letter, but contained the following postscript:

> Tsen Hing, the son of the Government schoolmaster,
> seems to be much in the company of your young wife.
> He is a good-looking youth, and pardon me, my dear
> cousin;—but if women are allowed to stray at will from
> under their husbands' mulberry roofs, what is to pre-
> vent them from becoming butterflies?

"Sing Foon is old and cynical," said Mr. Spring Fragrance to
himself. "Why should I pay any attention to him? This is America,
where a man may speak to a woman and a woman listen, without
any thought of evil."

He destroyed his cousin's letter and re-read his wife's. Then he
became very thoughtful. Was the making of American fudge sufficient reason for a wife to wish to remain a week longer in a city
where her husband was not?

The young man who lived in the next house came out to water
the lawn.

"Good evening," said he. "Any news from Mrs. Spring Fragrance?"

"She is having a very good time," returned Mr. Spring Fragrance.

"Glad to hear it. I think you told me she was to return the end
of this week."

"I have changed my mind about her," said Mr. Spring Fragrance.
"I am bidding her remain a week longer, as I wish to give a smoking
party during her absence. I hope I may have the pleasure of your
company."

"I shall be delighted," returned the young fellow. "But, Mr. Spring
Fragrance, don't invite any other white fellows. If you do not I shall
be able to get in a scoop. You know, I'm a sort of honorary reporter
for the Gleaner."

"Very well," absently answered Mr. Spring Fragrance.

"Of course, your friend the Consul will be present. I shall call it
'A highclass Chinese stag party!'"

In spite of his melancholy mood, Mr. Spring Fragrance smiled.

"Everything is 'high-class' in America," he observed.

"Sure!" cheerfully assented the young man. "Haven't you ever heard that all Americans are princes and princesses, and just as soon as a foreigner puts his foot upon our shores, he also becomes of the nobility—I mean, the royal family."

"What about my brother in the Detention Pen?" dryly inquired Mr. Spring Fragrance.

"Now, you've got me," said the young man, rubbing his head. "Well, that is a shame—'a beastly shame,' as the Englishman says. But understand, old fellow, we that are real Americans are up against that—even more than you. It is against our principles."

"I offer the real Americans my consolations that they should be compelled to do that which is against their principles."

"Oh, well, it will all come right some day. We're not a bad sort, you know. Think of the indemnity money returned to the Dragon by Uncle Sam."

Mr. Spring Fragrance puffed his pipe in silence for some moments. More than politics was troubling his mind.

At last he spoke. "Love," said he, slowly and distinctly, "comes before the wedding in this country; does it not?"

"Yes, certainly."

Young Carman knew Mr. Spring Fragrance well enough to receive with calmness his most astounding queries.

"Presuming," continued Mr. Spring Fragrance—"presuming that some friend of your father's, living—presuming—in England—has a daughter that he arranges with your father to be your wife. Presuming that you have never seen that daughter, but that you marry her, knowing her not. Presuming that she marries you, knowing you not.—After she marries you and knows you, will that woman love you?"

"Emphatically, no," answered the young man.

"That is the way it would be in America that the woman who

marries the man like that—would not love him?"

"Yes, that is the way it would be in America. Love, in this country, must be free, or it is not love at all."

"In China, it is different!" mused Mr. Spring Fragrance.

"Oh, yes, I have no doubt that in China it is different."

"But the love is in the heart all the same," went on Mr. Spring Fragrance.

"Yes, all the same. Everybody falls in love sometime or another. Some"—pensively—"many times."

Mr. Spring Fragrance arose.

"I must go down town," said he.

As he walked down the street he recalled the remark of a business acquaintance who had met his wife and had had some conversation with her: "She is just like an American woman."

He had felt somewhat flattered when this remark had been made. He looked upon it as a compliment to his wife's cleverness; but it rankled in his mind as he entered the telegraph office. If his wife was becoming as an American woman, would it not be possible for her to love as an American woman—a man to whom she was not married? There also floated in is memory the verse which his wife had quoted to the daughter of Chin Yuen. When the telegraph clerk handed him a blank, he wrote this message:

> Remain as you wish, but remember that "Tis better to have loved and lost, than never to have loved at all.'"

* * *

When Mrs. Spring Fragrance received this message, her laughter tinkled like falling water. How droll! How delightful! Here was her husband quoting American poetry in a telegram. Perhaps he had been reading her American poetry books since she had left him! She hoped so. They would lead him to understand her sympathy for her dear Laura and Kai Tzu. She need no longer keep from him their secret. How joyful! It had been such a hardship to refrain from confiding in him before. But discreetness had been most necessary, seeing that Mr. Spring Fragrance entertained as old-fashioned notions concerning marriage as did the Chin Yuen parents. Strange that that should be so, since he had fallen in love with her picture before ever he had seen her, just as she had fallen in love with his! And when the marriage veil was lifted and each beheld the other for the first time in the flesh, there had been no disillusion—no lessening of the respect and affection, which those who had brought about the marriage had inspired in each young heart.

Mrs. Spring Fragrance began to wish she could fall asleep and wake to find the week flown, and she in her own little home pouring tea for Mr. Spring Fragrance.

IV

Mr. Spring Fragrance was walking to business with Mr. Chin Yuen. As they walked they talked.

"Yes," said Mr. Chin Yuen, "the old order is passing away, and the new order is taking its place, even with us who are Chinese. I have finally consented to give my daughter in marriage to young Kai Tzu."

Mr. Spring Fragrance expressed surprise. He had understood that the marriage between his neighbor's daughter and the San Francisco schoolteacher's son was all arranged.

"So 'twas," answered Mr. Chin Yuen; "but it seems the young renegade, without consultation or advice, has placed his affections upon some untrustworthy female, and is so under her influence that he refuses to fulfil his parents' promise to me for him."

"So!" said Mr. Spring Fragrance. The shadow on his brow deepened.

"But," said Mr. Chin Yuen, with affable resignation, "it is all ordained by Heaven. Our daughter, as the wife of Kai Tzu, for whom she has long had a loving feeling, will not now be compelled to dwell with a mother-in-law and where her own mother is not. For that, we are thankful, as she is our only one and the conditions of life in this Western country are not as in China. Moreover, Kai Tzu, though not so much of a scholar as the teacher's son, has a keen eye for business and that, in America, is certainly much more desirable than scholarship. What do you think?"

"Eh! What!" exclaimed Mr. Spring Fragrance. The latter part of his companion's remarks had been lost upon him.

That day the shadow which had been following Mr. Spring Fragrance ever since he had heard his wife quote, "'Tis better to have loved," etc., became so heavy and deep that he quite lost himself within it.

At home in the evening he fed the cat, the bird, and the flowers. Then, seating himself in a carved black chair—a present from his wife on his last birthday—he took out his pipe and smoked. The cat jumped into his lap. He stroked it softly and tenderly. It had been much fondled by Mrs. Spring Fragrance, and Mr. Spring Fragrance was under the impression that it missed her. "Poor thing!" said he. "I suppose you want her back!" When he arose to go to bed he placed the animal carefully on the floor, and thus apostrophized it:

"O Wise and Silent One, your mistress returns to you, but her heart she leaves behind her, with the Tommies in San Francisco."

The Wise and Silent One made no reply. He was not a jealous cat.

Mr. Spring Fragrance slept not that night; the next morning he ate not. Three days and three nights without sleep and food went by.

There was a springlike freshness in the air on the day that Mrs. Spring Fragrance came home. The skies overhead were as blue as Puget Sound stretching its gleaming length toward the mighty Pacific, and all the beautiful green world seemed to be throbbing with springing life.

Mrs. Spring Fragrance was never so radiant.

"Oh," she cried light-heartedly, "is it not lovely to see the sun shining so clear, and everything so bright to welcome me?"

Mr. Spring Fragrance made no response. It was the morning after the fourth sleepless night.

Mrs. Spring Fragrance noticed his silence, also his grave face.

"Everything—everyone is glad to see me but you," she declared, half seriously, half jestingly.

Mr. Spring Fragrance set down her valise. They had just entered the house.

"If my wife is glad to see me," he quietly replied, "I also am glad to see her!"

Summoning their servant boy, he bade him look after Mrs. Spring Fragrance's comfort.

"I must be at the store in half an hour," said he, looking at his watch. "There is some very important business requiring attention."

"What is the business?" inquired Mrs. Spring Fragrance, her lip quivering with disappointment.

"I cannot just explain to you," answered her husband.

Mrs. Spring Fragrance looked up into his face with honest and earnest eyes. There was something in his manner, in the tone of her husband's voice, which touched her.

"Yen," said she, "you do not look well. You are not well. What is it?"

Something arose in Mr. Spring Fragrance's throat which prevented him from replying.

"O darling one! O sweetest one!" cried a girl's joyous voice. Laura Chin Yuen ran into the room and threw her arms around Mrs. Spring Fragrance's neck.

"I spied you from the window," said Laura, "and I couldn't rest until I told you. We are to be married next week, Kai Tzu and I. And all through you, all through you—the sweetest jade jewel in the world!"

Mr. Spring Fragrance passed out of the room.

"So the son of the Government teacher and little Happy Love are already married," Laura went on, relieving Mrs. Spring Fragrance of her cloak, her hat, and her folding fan.

Mr. Spring Fragrance paused upon the doorstep.

"Sit down, Little Sister, and I will tell you all about it," said Mrs. Spring Fragrance, forgetting her husband for a moment.

When Laura Chin Yuen had danced away, Mr. Spring Fragrance came in and hung up his hat.

"You got back very soon," said Mrs. Spring Fragrance, covertly wiping away the tears which had begun to fall as soon as she thought herself alone.

"I did not go," answered Mr. Spring Fragrance. "I have been listening to you and Laura."

"But if the business is very important, do not you think you should attend to it?" anxiously queried Mrs. Spring Fragrance.

"It is not important to me now," returned Mr. Spring Fragrance. "I would prefer to hear again about Ah Oi and Man You and Laura and Kai Tzu."

"How lovely of you to say that!" exclaimed Mrs. Spring Fragrance, who was easily made happy. And she began to chat away to her husband in the friendliest and wifeliest fashion possible. When she had finished she asked him if he were not glad to hear that those who loved as did the young lovers whose secrets she had been keeping, were to be united; and he replied that indeed he was; that he would like every man to be as happy with a wife as he himself had ever been and ever would be.

"You did not always talk like that," said Mrs. Spring Fragrance slyly. "You must have been reading my American poetry books!"

"American poetry!" ejaculated Mr. Spring Fragrance almost fiercely, "American poetry is detestable, *abhorrable*!"

"Why! why!" exclaimed Mrs. Spring Fragrance, more and more surprised.

But the only explanation which Mr. Spring Fragrance vouchsafed was a jadestone pendant.

MISS FURR AND MISS SKEENE[1]

Gertrude Stein

HELEN FURR HAD quite a pleasant home. Mrs. Furr was quite a pleasant woman. Mr. Furr was quite a pleasant man. Helen Furr had quite a pleasant voice a voice quite worth cultivating. She did not mind working. She worked to cultivate her voice. She did not find it gay living in the same place where she had always been living. She went to a place where some were cultivating something, voices and other things needing cultivating. She met Georgine Skeene there who was cultivating her voice which some thought was quite a pleasant one. Helen Furr and Georgine Skeene lived together then. Georgine Skeene liked travelling. Helen Furr did not care about travelling, she liked to stay in one place and be gay there. They were together then and travelled to another place and stayed there and were gay there.

They stayed there and were gay there, not very gay there, just gay there. They were both gay there, they were regularly working there both of them cultivating their voices there, they were both gay there. Georgine Skeene was gay there and she was regular, regular in being gay, regular in not being gay, regular in being a gay one who was one not being gay longer than was needed to be one being quite a gay one. They were both gay then there and both working there then.

They were in a way both gay there where there were many cultivating something. They were both regular in being gay there. Helen

1   First published in Gertrude Stein, *Geography and Plays* (Boston: The Four Seas Press, 1922).

Furr was gay there, she was gayer and gayer there and really she was just gay there, she was gayer and gayer there, that is to say she found ways of being gay there that she was using in being gay there. She was gay there, not gayer and gayer, just gay there, that is to say she was not gayer by using the things she found there that were gay things, she was gay there, always she was gay there.

They were quite regularly gay there, Helen Furr and Georgine Skeene, they were regularly gay there where they were gay. They were very regularly gay.

To be regularly gay was to do every day the gay thing that they did every day. To be regularly gay was to end every day at the same time after they had been regularly gay. They were regularly gay. They were gay every day. They ended every day in the same way, at the same time, and they had been every day regularly gay.

The voice Helen Furr was cultivating was quite a pleasant one. The voice Georgine Skeene was cultivating was, some said, a better one. The voice Helen Furr was cultivating she cultivated and it was quite completely a pleasant enough one then, a cultivated enough one then. The voice Georgine Skeene was cultivating she did not cultivate too much. She cultivated it quite some. She cultivated and she would sometime go on cultivating it and it was not then an unpleasant one, it would not be then an unpleasant one, it would be a quite richly enough cultivated one, it would be quite richly enough to be a pleasant enough one.

They were gay where there were many cultivating something. The two were gay there, were regularly gay there. Georgine Skeene would have liked to do more travelling. They did some travelling, not very much travelling, Georgine Skeene would have liked to do more travelling, Helen Furr did not care about doing travelling, she liked to stay in a place and be gay there.

They stayed in a place and were gay there, both of them stayed there, they stayed together there, they were gay there, they were regularly gay there.

They went quite often, not very often, but they did go back to where Helen Furr had a pleasant enough home and then Georgine Skeene went to a place where her brother had quite some distinction. They both went, every few years, went visiting to where Helen Furr had quite a pleasant home. Certainly Helen Furr would not find it gay to stay, she did not find it gay, she said she would not stay, she said she did not find it gay, she said she would not stay where she did not find it gay, she said she found it gay where she did stay and she did stay there where very many were cultivating something. She did stay there. She always did find it gay there.

She went to see them where she had always been living and where she did not find it gay. She had a pleasant home there, Mrs. Furr was a pleasant enough woman, Mr. Furr was a pleasant enough man, Helen told them and they were not worrying, that she did not find it gay living where she had always been living.

Georgine Skeene and Helen Furr were living where they were both cultivating their voices and they were gay there. They visited where Helen Furr had come from and then they went to where they were living where they were then regularly living.

There were some dark and heavy men there then. There were some who were not so heavy and some who were not so dark. Helen Furr and Georgine Skeene sat regularly with them. They sat regularly with the ones who were dark and heavy. They sat regularly with the ones who were not so dark. They sat regularly with the ones that were not so heavy. They sat with them regularly, sat with some of them. They went with them regularly went with them. They were regular then, they were gay then, they were where they wanted to be then where it was gay to be then, they were regularly gay then. There were men there then who were dark and heavy and they sat with them with Helen Furr and Georgine Skeene and they went with them with Miss Furr and Miss Skeene, and they went with the heavy and dark men Miss Furr and Miss Skeene went with them, and they sat with them, Miss Furr and Miss Skeene sat with them,

and there were other men, some were not heavy men and they sat
with Miss Furr and Miss Skeene and Miss Furr and Miss Skeene sat
with them, and there were other men who were not dark men and
they sat with Miss Furr and Miss Skeene and Miss Furr and Miss
Skeene sat with them. Miss Furr and Miss Skeene went with them
and they went with Miss Furr and Miss Skeene, some who were
not heavy men, some who were not dark men. Miss Furr and Miss
Skeene sat regularly, they sat with some men. Miss Furr and Miss
Skeene went and there were some men with them. There were men
and Miss Furr and Miss Skeene went with them, went somewhere
with them, went with some of them.

Helen Furr and Georgine Skeene were regularly living where
very many were living and cultivating in themselves something.
Helen Furr and Georgine Skeene were living very regularly then,
being very regular then in being gay then. They did then learn
many ways to be gay and they were then being gay being quite regular in being gay, being gay and they were learning little things,
little things in ways of being gay, they were very regular then, they
were learning very many little things in ways of being gay, they were
being gay and using these little things they were learning to have
to be gay with regularly gay with then and they were gay the same
amount they had been gay. They were quite gay, they were quite
regular, they were learning little things, gay little things, they were
gay inside them the same amount they had been gay, they were gay
the same length of time they had been gay every day.

They were regular in being gay, they learned little things that are
things in being gay, they learned many little things that are things
in being gay, they were gay every day, they were regular, they were
gay, they were gay the same length of time every day, they were gay,
they were quite regularly gay.

Georgine Skeene went away to stay two months with her brother.
Helen Furr did not go then to stay with her father and her mother.
Helen Furr stayed there where they had been regularly living the

two of them and she would then certainly not be lonesome, she would go on being gay. She did go on being gay. She was not any more gay but she was gay longer every day than they had been being gay when they were together being gay. She was gay then quite exactly the same way. She learned a few more little ways of being in being gay. She was quite gay and in the same way, the same way she had been gay and she was gay a little longer in the day, more of each day she was gay. She was gay longer every day than when the two of them had been being gay. She was gay quite in the way they had been gay, quite in the same way.

She was not lonesome then, she was not at all feeling any need of having Georgine Skeene. She was not astonished at this thing. She would have been a little astonished by this thing but she knew she was not astonished at anything and so she was not astonished at this thing not astonished at not feeling any need of having Georgine Skeene.

Helen Furr had quite a completely pleasant voice and it was quite well enough cultivated and she could use it and she did use it but then there was not any way of working at cultivating a completely pleasant voice when it has become a quite completely well enough cultivated one, and there was not much use in using it when one was not wanting it to be helping to make one a gay one. Helen Furr was not needing using her voice to be a gay one. She was gay then and sometimes she used her voice and she was not using it very often. It was quite completely enough cultivated and it was quite completely a pleasant one and she did not use it very often. She was then, she was quite exactly as gay as she had been, she was gay a little longer in the day than she had been.

She was gay exactly the same way. She was never tired of being gay that way. She had learned very many little ways to use in being gay. Very many were telling about using other ways in being gay. She was gay enough, she was always gay exactly the same way, she was always learning little things to use in being gay, she was telling about using other ways in being gay, she was telling about learning other ways in being gay, she was learning other ways in being gay, she would be using other ways in being gay, she would always be gay in the same way, when Georgine Skeene was there not so long each day as when Georgine Skeene was away.

She came to using many ways in being gay, she came to use every way in being gay. She went on living where many were cultivating something and she was gay, she had used every way to be gay.

They did not live together then Helen Furr and Georgine Skeene. Helen Furr lived there the longer where they had been living regularly together. Then neither of them were living there any longer. Helen Furr was living somewhere else then and telling some about being gay and she was gay then and she was living quite regularly then. She was regularly gay then. She was quite regular in being gay then. She remembered all the little ways of being gay. She used all the little ways of being gay. She was quite regularly gay. She told many then the way of being gay, she taught very many then little ways they could use in being gay. She was living very well, she was gay then, she went on living then, she was regular in being gay, she always was living very well and was gay very well and was telling about little ways one could be learning to use in being gay, and later was telling them quite often, telling them again and again.

WHAT DO YOU SEE, MADAM?[1]

Djuna Barnes

MAMIE SALOAM WAS a dancer.

She had come from the lower stratum of the poor, who drape their shoulders with cotton and their stomachs with gingham.

The Bowery, which is no place at all for virtue or duplicity, had seen Mamie try on her first fit of sulks and her first stay laces. They knew then that her pattern was Juno, her heritage Joseph, and her ambition jade. At the age of ten she had learned to interpret Oscar Wilde, when Oscar Wilde had gone in, rather extensively, for passion and the platter, and had parried off creation with a movement and a beard.

On that moonlit night, when she chucked Semco, the sailor, under the chin, and swiped one of the park lilacs for keeps, Mamie grew up.

Between his lips and hers she had learned competition. His was the greater kiss, his arms the greater strength, his voice the master voice.

Mamie became fire and felt hell where it burns low among the coals, and the street that sensed her homecoming on staccato heels heard the wide-mouthed laughter she threw her mother as she rolled into bed.

Thereafter she swore that her life should be given to portraying detached emotions, to placing love on the boards. Her ambition was to kiss the lips of John the Baptist as they lay in plaster glory upon a little tin plate.

---

1   First published in *All-Story Cavalier Weekly*, XLIII (March 27, 1915).

When a subaltern puts his head under cover, he is a coward. When Mamie Saloam sought the underside of the counterpane, she was merely looking for future ethics.

Mamie twisted the Bowery out of her air, threw her hips into the maelstrom of rightly moving things, and raised an organism of potato and cod to the level of caviar and champagne. When she turned about, she had taken three steps in the direction of the proverbial gentleman who follows after the world and the flesh.

The rich and the poor are divided only in the matter of scorn: eye scorn, lip scorn, and the sudden rude laughter that runs the gamut of Broadway. All these leaped into Mamie's saucy face as she looked at herself for the first time in a mirror that gave her back, whole.

When she walked out, one heard only the sound of slum slippers and the regular cadence of her knees as she descended the steps. She was used to uneven footing.

After the mirror she swore that she had taken the last cod bone from between her teeth and now she would chew only after-dinner mints.

When a girl gives up gum and alleys, and has known little else, she becomes something different, and the something different that Mamie became was a dancer, toe and otherwise.

Into the little world of the painted came Mamie. Into that place of press-agents and powder-puffs, of Lillian Russell and Raymond Hitchcock, of Irving and of Sarah, scented with lilac and Bel Bon, throbbing and pulsating with the sound of laughter; into that little stall called the dressing room, out of which none may come unchanged.

Mamie Saloam was a good medium on which to lay cosmetics. Everything merely accentuated those points that God and the Saloams had given her; in fact, the teamwork between the two had been sublime. Mamie was beautiful.

She was loved by the men down front because she had mastered the technique of the tights.

Her world held rows and rows of dusty caned chairs, and over these, like migrating robins, the pink anatomy of the chorus—hips thrown out against the painted drop, listless eyes that saw only supper, a new step, and once in a while, some other things. Mamie Saloam could go where she willed. She could stoop or look up because Mamie breathed true ambition and heroic drudgery.

When she passed the boundaries of decency, it was a full run for your money; when she went up in smoke, those original little pasty pans of Egypt became chimney pots. If Helen of Troy could have been seen eating peppermints out of a paper bag, it is highly probable that her admirers would have been an entirely different class.

It is the thing you are found doing while the horde looks on that you shall be loved for—or ignored.

Billy had caught Mamie pinning "Thou shalt not sin" up high on the door of her room in the house of chameleon thoughts. He then knew—for even electricians can know things—that the way to approach Mamie was to sit close and abide in hope, for opportunity comes once to every man.

While he waited, Mamie made up her one philosophy. It was made, of course, for the benefit of women. It read: "A woman never knows what she sees, therefore, she tries to see what she knows."

"Listen," said the stage manager one night from out of the gloom where Mamie sat restringing the beads that passed for combinations, underskirt, shift petticoat, bodice skirt, and withal, propriety for Salome. "Listen, we are in a fix. The P.I.B. is on to us and you."

"In what way?" inquired Mamie Saloam.

"They have gotten on to the fact that early in the season we are to present you as *Salomé*. They have prejudices—"

"Of course they have," said Mamie calmly; "they have seen Mme. Aguglia, Mary Garden, Gertrude Hoffman, and Trixie Friganza do the stunt; they have all seen what they wanted to see because the aforesaid showed them what they wanted to see. I'll admit that John hasn't been properly loved since the original gurgle ceased; I'll admit that as we have gotten further and further away from the real head, we have dealt with rather papier-mâché passions.

"John was rather lethargic in his response even in the beginning, and we have made too much fuss over him. When a man is dead, a certain respect is due him; it is a proper and a joyous thing to dance about him, but I do think he has been rather overkissed. I will show the ladies of the P.I.B. the necessary moderation, even if the gentleman is helpless. Leave it to me."

"By the way," she added as the stage manager pondered, his hand in his hair, "what is the P.I.B.?"

"It is the Prevention of Impurities upon the Boards," he said, and smiled at her.

"And what do they want?"

"They either want the performance stopped or—they want to see a purely impartial rendering."

Billy looked at her from beneath his shaggy eyebrows. Then suddenly he let go of the thing that is called reserve and took her hand.

"Mamie," he said, "couldn't you respond to me; couldn't I ever be anything to you; couldn't I make up for all this"—he waved his arm broadcast—"this ambition stuff?"

"Billy," she said, and her voice was cold and practical, "I couldn't ever boil potatoes over the heat of your affection. Your love would never bridge a gap; it wouldn't even fill up the hole that the mice came through, and," she concluded, withdrawing her hand, "I couldn't ever consider anyone less than John."

Deep down in Billy's heart lay a terrible passion that itched to force this allegorical obstacle from between him and the woman. As he sat in his perch up in the wings and focused the blue light upon the platter and the white upturned plaster face, he knew what had put the word "La mort" into the dictionary and into circulation, and he groaned within his soul.

The next day they took away the dusty rows of chairs, the heaps of discarded tights, shed by human butterflies that had grown into something more brilliant or had died emerging from the chrysalis prematurely. They did not notice that it was dusty until they saw two spots some three inches apart, which looked as if someone had fallen upon his knees.

They did not speculate any further, but Mamie saw.

The stage hands cleaned and fussed in preparation for the trial scene to be given for the benefit of the P.I.B. A pitcher, belonging to the dresser, very much cracked, and yet gaudy as the owner, was filled with lemonade, which first frosted the outside like a young woman's demeanor when holding the young man off, and finally broke out into great beads and slid over the hips of the pitcher to the table below like the tears that follow up the first grief.

It was quite dark back stage when they were through. The little bags of ballast that let down Florida or France from the ceiling hung swaying fifty feet above Billy as he tinkered with the lights.

Out front sat the stage manager between the starched ladies of the P.I.B., drinking the lemonade gently yet firmly from tall, frail glasses. They looked at each other across the chain-encircled vest of the stage manager with the macaw look which is strictly limited to boards of prevention and committees for inspection.

They would like to think well of Mamie Saloam, but as Mamie said, they had seen Mme. Aguglia.

Then out across the dusky stage came Mamie, tall and dominating. Her bare shoulders supported vivid streams of her hair.

For a minute she stood poised in the center of the stage, a voluptuous outline in the mist.

Then the spotlight fell, not upon Mamie, but upon the face of John, upturned and white, with half-closed lids, the hair and beard flowing over the edge of the plate. Dark loops broke the dead white of the forehead, a silent questioning of the painted lips awaiting the performance of Mamie Saloam, who had learned to kiss ten years before.

The ladies of the P.I.B., not to be fooled, leaned sternly over their glasses. They wanted to be sure that there was a simplicity in the way Mamie Saloam wallowed before her lord.

On she came, halting, and then suddenly broke into a semicircle of half-steps about the head of the dead Baptist, gurgling, throaty little noises escaping her lips. Slowly she lowered herself until, imperceptibly to the starched ladies, she lay upon the floor and sinuously wriggled toward the tin platter.

Sidewise, forward, approaching it with plastic hands, nearer and nearer and nearer till the platter was within the zone of her very breath. Over it she hovered, murmuring, while her eyes changed from blue to green and from green to deep opal. Then suddenly she dropped her chin among the strands of the flowing beard.

The starched ladies sighed and relaxed. Here was a woman at last who could do the thing with perfect impartiality. They turned approving eyes upon the manager.

"She has John under perfect control," they said, and passed out.

Then Mamie did a strange thing. She sat up, put her arms about her knees, and looked serenely at the face still motionless in the blue of the light from the unoccupied electrician's box. John the Baptist batted his right eye.

"Get up, Billy," she said. "It's all right. Let us thank the dark of a back stage night, and your ability to lie still. At last I have proved that a woman never knows what she is seeing."

SWEAT[1]

Zora Neale Hurston

It was eleven o'clock of a Spring night in Florida. It was Sunday. Any other night, Delia Jones would have been in bed for two hours by this time. But she was a wash-woman, and Monday morning meant a great deal to her. So she collected the soiled clothes on Saturday when she returned the clean things. Sunday night after church, she sorted them and put the white things to soak. It saved her almost a half day's start. A great hamper in the bedroom held the clothes that she brought home. It was so much neater than a number of bundles lying around.

She squatted in the kitchen floor beside the great pile of clothes, sorting them into small heaps according to color, and humming a song in a mournful key, but wondering through it all where Sykes, her husband, had gone with her horse and buckboard.

Just then something long, round, limp and black fell upon her shoulders and slithered to the floor beside her. A great terror took hold of her. It softened her knees and dried her mouth so that it was a full minute before she could cry out or move. Then she saw that it was the big bull whip her husband liked to carry when he drove.

She lifted her eyes to the door and saw him standing there bent over with laughter at her fright. She screamed at him.

"Sykes, what you throw dat whip on me like dat? You know it would skeer me—looks just like a snake, an' you knows how skeered Ah is of snakes."

1   First published in *Fire!!* (magazine) ed. by Wallace Thurman, in association with Langston Hughes, Gwendolyn Bennett, Richard Bruce, Zora Neale Hurston, Aaron Douglas, John Davis (New York: November 1926).

"Course Ah knowed it! That's how come Ah done it." He slapped his leg with his hand and almost rolled on the ground in his mirth. "If you such a big fool dat you got to have a fit over a earth worm or a string, Ah don't keer how bad Ah skeer you."

"You aint got no business doing it. Gawd knows it's a sin. Some day Ah'm goin' tuh drop dead from some of yo' foolishness. 'Nother thing, where you been wid mah rig? Ah feeds dat pony. He aint fuh you to be drivin' wid no bull whip."

"You sho is one aggravatin' nigger woman!" he declared and stepped into the room. She resumed her work and did not answer him at once. "Ah done tole you time and again to keep them white folks' clothes outa dis house."

He picked up the whip and glared down at her. Delia went on with her work. She went out into the yard and returned with a galvanized tub and set it on the washbench. She saw that Sykes had kicked all of the clothes together again, and now stood in her way truculently, his whole manner hoping, *praying*, for an argument. But she walked calmly around him and commenced to re-sort the things.

"Next time, Ah'm gointer kick 'em outdoors," he threatened as he struck a match along the leg of his corduroy breeches.

Delia never looked up from her work, and her thin, stooped shoulders sagged further.

"Ah aint for no fuss t'night Sykes. Ah just come from taking sacrament at the church house."

He snorted scornfully. "Yeah, you just come from de church house on a Sunday night, but heah you is gone to work on them clothes. You ain't nothing but a hypocrite. One of them amen-corner Christians—sing, whoop, and shout, then come home and wash white folks clothes on the Sabbath."

He stepped roughly upon the whitest pile of things, kicking them helter-skelter as he crossed the room. His wife gave a little scream of dismay, and quickly gathered them together again.

"Sykes, you quit grindin' dirt into these clothes! How can Ah git through by Sat'day if Ah don't start on Sunday?"

"Ah don't keer if you never git through. Anyhow, Ah done promised Gawd and a couple of other men, Ah aint gointer have it in mah house. Don't gimme no lip neither, else Ah'll throw 'em out and put mah fist up side yo' head to boot."

Delia's habitual meekness seemed to slip from her shoulders like a blown scarf. She was on her feet; her poor little body, her bare knuckly hands bravely defying the strapping hulk before her.

"Looka heah, Sykes, you done gone too fur. Ah been married to you fur fifteen years, and Ah been takin' in washin' for fifteen years. Sweat, sweat, sweat! Work and sweat, cry and sweat, pray and sweat!"

"What's that got to do with me?" he asked brutally.

"What's it got to do with you, Sykes? Mah tub of suds is filled yo' belly with vittles more times than yo' hands is filled it. Mah sweat is done paid for this house and Ah reckon Ah kin keep on sweatin' in it."

She seized the iron skillet from the stove and struck a defensive pose, which act surprised him greatly, coming from her. It cowed him and he did not strike her as he usually did.

"Naw you won't," she panted, "that ole snaggle-toothed black woman you runnin' with aint comin' heah to pile up on *mah* sweat and blood. You aint paid for nothin' on this place, and Ah'm gointer stay right heah till Ah'm toted out foot foremost."

"Well, you better quit gittin' me riled up, else they'll be totin' you out sooner than you expect. Ah'm so tired of you Ah don't know whut to do. Gawd! how Ah hates skinny wimmen!"

A little awed by this new Delia, he sidled out of the door and slammed the back gate after him. He did not say where he had gone, but she knew too well. She knew very well that he would not return until nearly daybreak also. Her work over, she went on to bed but not to sleep at once. Things had come to a pretty pass!

She lay awake, gazing upon the debris that cluttered their mat-
rimonial trail. Not an image left standing along the way. Anything
like flowers had long ago been drowned in the salty stream that
had been pressed from her heart. Her tears, her sweat, her blood.
She had brought love to the union and he had brought a longing
after the flesh. Two months after the wedding, he had given her the
first brutal beating. She had the memory of his numerous trips to
Orlando with all of his wages when he had returned to her penniless, even before the first year had passed. She was young and
soft then, but now she thought of her knotty, muscled limbs, her
harsh knuckly hands, and drew herself up into an unhappy little
ball in the middle of the big feather bed. Too late now to hope for
love, even if it were not Bertha it would be someone else. This case
differed from the others only in that she was bolder than the others.
Too late for everything except her little home. She had built it for
her old days, and planted one by one the trees and flowers there. It
was lovely to her, lovely.

Somehow, before sleep came, she found herself saying aloud:
"Oh well, whatever goes over the Devil's back, is got to come under
his belly. Sometime or ruther, Sykes, like everybody else, is gointer
reap his sowing." After that she was able to build a spiritual earth-
works against her husband. His shells could no longer reach her.
Amen. She went to sleep and slept until he announced his presence
in bed by kicking her feet and rudely snatching the covers away.

"Gimme some kivah heah, an' git yo' damn foots over on yo' own
side! Ah oughter mash you in yo' mouf fuh drawing dat skillet on
me."

Delia went clear to the rail without answering him. A triumphant
indifference to all that he was or did.

* * *

The week was as full of work for Delia as all other weeks, and

Saturday found her behind her little pony, collecting and delivering clothes.

It was a hot, hot day near the end of July. The village men on Joe Clarke's porch even chewed cane listlessly. They did not hurl the cane-knots as usual. They let them dribble over the edge of the porch. Even conversation had collapsed under the heat.

"Heah come Delia Jones," Jim Merchant said, as the shaggy pony came 'round the bend of the road toward them. The rusty buckboard was heaped with baskets of crisp, clean laundry.

"Yep," Joe Lindsay agreed. "Hot or col', rain or shine, jes ez reg'lar ez de weeks roll roun' Delia carries 'em an' fetches 'em on Sat'day."

"She better if she wanter eat," said Moss. "Syke Jones aint wuth de shot an' powder hit would tek tuh kill 'em. Not to *huh* he aint."

"He sho' aint," Walter Thomas chimed in. "It's too bad, too, cause she wuz a right pritty lil trick when he got huh. Ah'd uh mah'ied huh mahseff if he hadnter beat me to it."

Delia nodded briefly at the men as she drove past.

"Too much knockin' will ruin *any* 'oman. He done beat huh 'nough tuh kill three women, let 'lone change they looks," said Elijah Moseley. "How Syke kin stommuck dat big black greasy Mogul he's layin' roun' wid, gits me. Ah swear dat eight-rock couldn't kiss a sardine can Ah done throwed out de back do' 'way las' yeah."

"Aw, she's fat, thass how come. He's allus been crazy 'bout fat women," put in Merchant. "He'd a' been tied up wid one long time ago if he could a' found one tuh have him. Did Ah tell yuh 'bout him come sidlin' roun' *mah* wife—bringin' her a basket uh pee-cans outa his yard fuh a present? Yessir, mah wife! She tol' him tuh take 'em right straight back home, cause Delia works so hard ovah dat washtub she reckon everything on de place taste lak sweat an' soap-suds. Ah jus' wisht Ah'd a' caught 'im 'dere! Ah'd a' made his hips ketch on fiah down dat shell road."

"Ah know he done it, too. Ah sees 'im grinnin' at every 'oman dat passes," Walter Thomas said. "But even so, he useter eat some mighty big hunks uh humble pie tuh git dat lil 'oman he got. She wuz ez pritty ez a speckled pup! Dat wuz fifteen yeahs ago. He useter be so skeered uh losin' huh, she could make him do some parts of a husband's duty. Dey never wuz de same in de mind."

"There oughter be a law about him," said Lindsay. "He aint fit tuh carry guts tuh a bear."

Clarke spoke for the first time. "Taint no law on earth dat kin make a man be decent if it aint in 'im. There's plenty men dat takes a wife lak dey do a joint uh sugar-cane. It's round, juicy an' sweet when dey gits it. But dey squeeze an' grind, squeeze an' grind an' wring tell dey wring every drop uh pleasure dat's in 'em out. When dey's satisfied dat dey is wrung dry, dey treats 'em jes lak dey do a cane-chew. Dey throws em away. Dey knows whut dey is doin' while dey is at it, an' hates theirselves fuh it but they keeps on hangin' after huh tell she's empty. Den dey hates huh fuh bein' a cane-chew an' in de way."

"We oughter take Syke an' dat stray 'oman uh his'n down in Lake Howell swamp an' lay on de rawhide till they cain't say 'Lawd a' mussy.' He allus wuz uh ovahbearin' niggah, but since dat white 'oman from up north done teached 'im how to run a automobile, he done got too biggety to live—an' we oughter kill 'im," Old Man Anderson advised.

A grunt of approval went around the porch. But the heat was melting their civic virtue, and Elijah Moseley began to bait Joe Clarke.

"Come on, Joe, git a melon outa dere an' slice it up for yo' customers. We'se all sufferin' wid de heat. De bear's done got *me*!"

"Thass right, Joe, a watermelon is jes' whut Ah needs tuh cure de eppizudicks," Walter Thomas joined forces with Moseley. "Come on dere, Joe. We all is steady customers an' you aint set us up in a long time. Ah chooses dat long, bowlegged Floridy favorite."

"A god, an' be dough. You all gimme twenty cents and slice way,"

Clarke retorted. "Ah needs a col' slice m'self. Heah, everybody chip in. Ah'll lend y'll mah meat knife."

The money was quickly subscribed and the huge melon brought forth. At that moment, Sykes and Bertha arrived. A determined silence fell on the porch and the melon was put away again.

Merchant snapped down the blade of his jackknife and moved toward the store door.

"Come on in, Joe, an' gimme a slab uh sow belly an' uh pound uh coffee—almost fuhgot 'twas Sat'day. Got to git on home." Most of the men left also.

Just then Delia drove past on her way home, as Sykes was ordering magnificently for Bertha. It pleased him for Delia to see.

"Git whutsoever yo' heart desires, Honey. Wait a minute, Joe. Give huh two bottles uh strawberry soda-water, uh quart uh parched ground-peas, an' a block uh chewin' gum."

With all this they left the store, with Sykes reminding Bertha that this was his town and she could have it if she wanted it.

The men returned soon after they left, and held their watermelon feast.

"Where did Syke Jones git da 'oman from nohow?" Lindsay asked.

"Ovah Apopka. Guess dey musta been cleanin' out de town when she lef'. She don't look lak a thing but a hunk uh liver wid hair on it."

"Well, she sho' kin squall," Dave Carter contributed. "When she gits ready tuh laff, she jes' opens huh mouf an' latches it back tuh de las' notch. No ole grandpa alligator down in Lake Bell ain't got nothin' on huh."

* * *

Bertha had been in town three months now. Sykes was still paying her room rent at Della Lewis'—the only house in town that would have taken her in. Sykes took her frequently to Winter Park to "stomps." He still assured her that he was the swellest man in the state.

"Sho' you kin have dat lil' ole house soon's Ah kin git dat 'oman outa dere. Everything b'longs tuh me an' you sho' kin have it. Ah sho' 'bominates uh skinny 'oman. Lawdy, you sho' is got one portly shape on you! You kin git *anything* you wants. Dis is *mah* town an' you sho' kin have it."

Delia's work-worn knees crawled over the earth in Gethsemane and up the rocks of Calvary many, many times during these months. She avoided the villagers and meeting places in her efforts to be blind and deaf. But Bertha nullified this to a degree, by coming to Delia's house to call Sykes out to her at the gate.

Delia and Sykes fought all the time now with no peaceful interludes. They slept and ate in silence. Two or three times Delia had attempted a timid friendliness, but she was repulsed each time. It was plain that the breaches must remain agape.

* * *

The sun had burned July to August. The heat streamed down like a million hot arrows, smiting all things living upon the earth. Grass withered, leaves browned, snakes went blind in shedding and men and dogs went mad. Dog days!

Delia came home one day and found Sykes there before her. She wondered, but started to go on into the house without speaking, even though he was standing in the kitchen door and she must either stoop under his arm or ask him to move. He made no room for her. She noticed a soap box beside the steps, but paid no particular attention to it, knowing that he must have brought it there. As she was stooping to pass under his outstretched arm, he suddenly pushed her backward, laughingly.

"Look in de box dere Delia, Ah done brung yuh somethin'!"

She nearly fell upon the box in her stumbling, and when she saw what it held, she all but fainted outright.

"Syke! Syke, mah Gawd! You take dat rattlesnake 'way from heah! You *gottuh*. Oh, Jesus, have mussy!"

"Ah aint gut tuh do nuthin' uh de kin'—fact is Ah aint got tuh do nothin' but die. Taint no use uh you puttin' on airs makin' out lak you skeered uh dat snake—he's gointer stay right heah tell he die. He wouldn't bite me cause Ah knows how tuh handle 'im. Nohow he wouldn't risk breakin' out his fangs 'gin *yo'* skinny laigs."

"Naw, now Syke, don't keep dat thing 'roun' heah tuh skeer me tuh death. You knows Ah'm even feared uh earth worms. Thass de biggest snake Ah evah did see. Kill 'im Syke, please."

"Doan ast me tuh do nothin' fuh yuh. Goin' roun' tryin' tuh be so damn asterperious. Naw, Ah aint gonna kill it. Ah think uh damn sight mo' uh him dan you! Dat's a nice snake an' anybody doan lak 'im kin jes' hit de grit."

The village soon heard that Sykes had the snake, and came to see and ask questions.

"How de hen-fire did you ketch dat six-foot rattler, Syke?" Thomas asked.

"He's full uh frogs so he caint hardly move, thass how. Ah eased up on 'm. But Ah'm a snake charmer an' knows how tuh handle 'em. Shux, dat aint nothin'. Ah could ketch one eve'y day if Ah so wanted tuh."

"Whut he needs is a heavy hick'ry club leaned real heavy on his head. Dat's de bes 'way tuh charm a rattlesnake."

"Naw, Walt, y'll jes' don't understand dese diamon' backs lak Ah do," said Sykes in a superior tone of voice.

The village agreed with Walter, but the snake stayed on. His box remained by the kitchen door with its screen wire covering. Two or three days later it had digested its meal of frogs and literally came to life. It rattled at every movement in the kitchen or the yard. One day as Delia came down the kitchen steps she saw his chalky-white fangs curved like scimitars hung in the wire meshes. This time she did not run away with averted eyes as usual. She stood for a long time in the doorway in a red fury that grew bloodier for every second that she regarded the creature that was her torment.

That night she broached the subject as soon as Sykes sat down to the table.

"Syke, Ah wants you tuh take dat snake 'way fum heah. You done starved me an' Ah put up widcher, you done beat me an Ah took dat, but you done kilt all mah insides bringin' dat varmint heah."

Sykes poured out a saucer full of coffee and drank it deliberately before he answered her.

"A whole lot Ah keer 'bout how you feels inside uh out. Dat snake aint goin' no damn wheah till Ah gits ready fuh 'im tuh go. So fur as beatin' is concerned, yuh aint took near all dat you gointer take ef yuh stay 'roun' *me*."

Delia pushed back her plate and got up from the table. "Ah hates you, Sykes," she said calmly. "Ah hates you tuh de same degree dat Ah useter love yuh. Ah done took an' took till mah belly is full up tuh mah neck. Dat's de reason Ah got mah letter fum de church an' moved mah membership tuh Woodbridge—so Ah don't haf tuh take no sacrament wid yuh. Ah don't wantuh see yuh 'roun' me atall. Lay 'roun' wid dat 'oman all yuh wants tuh, but gwan 'way fum me an' mah house. Ah hates yuh lak uh suck-egg dog."

Sykes almost let the huge wad of corn bread and collard greens he was chewing fall out of his mouth in amazement. He had a hard time whipping himself up to the proper fury to try to answer Delia.

"Well, Ah'm glad you does hate me. Ah'm sho' tiahed uh you hangin' ontuh me. Ah don't want yuh. Look at yuh stringey ole neck! Yo' rawbony laigs an' arms is enough tuh cut uh man tuh death. You looks jes' lak de devvul's doll-baby tuh *me*. You cain't hate me no worse dan Ah hates you. Ah been hatin' *you* fuh years."

"Yo' ole black hide don't look lak nothin' tuh me, but uh passle uh wrinkled up rubber, wid yo' big ole yeahs flappin' on each side lak uh paih uh buzzard wings. Don't think Ah'm gointuh be run 'way fum mah house neither. Ah'm goin' tuh de white folks bout *you*, mah young man, de very nex' time you lay yo' han's on me. Mah cup is done run ovah." Delia said this with no signs of fear and Sykes departed from the house, threatening her, but made not the slightest move to carry out any of them.

That night he did not return at all, and the next day being Sunday, Delia was glad she did not have to quarrel before she hitched up her pony and drove the four miles to Woodbridge.

She stayed to the night service—"love feast"—which was very warm and full of spirit. In the emotional winds her domestic trials were borne far and wide so that she sang as she drove homeward.

> "*Jurden water, black an' col'*
> *Chills de body, not de soul*
> *An' Ah wantah cross Jurden in uh calm time.*"

She came from the barn to the kitchen door and stopped.

"Whut's de mattah, ol' satan, you aint kickin' up yo' racket?" She addressed the snake's box. Complete silence. She went on into the house with a new hope in its birth struggles. Perhaps her threat to go to the white folks had frightened Sykes! Perhaps he was sorry! Fifteen years of misery and suppression had brought Delia to the place where she would hope *anything* that looked towards a way over or through her wall of inhibitions.

She felt in the match safe behind the stove at once for a match. There was only one there.

"Dat niggah wouldn't fetch nothin' heah tuh save his rotten neck, but he kin run thew whut Ah brings quick enough. Now he done toted off nigh on tuh haff uh box uh matches. He done had dat 'oman heah in mah house, too."

Nobody but a woman could tell how she knew this even before she struck the match. But she did and it put her into a new fury.

Presently she brought in the tubs to put the white things to soak. This time she decided she need not bring the hamper out of the bedroom; she would go in there and do the sorting. She picked up the pot-bellied lamp and went in. The room was small and the hamper stood hard by the foot of the white iron bed. She could sit and reach through the bedposts—resting as she worked.

"Ah wantah cross Jurden in uh calm time," she was singing again. The mood of the "love feast" had returned. She threw back the lid of the basket almost gaily. Then, moved by both horror and terror, she sprang back toward the door. *There lay the snake in the basket!* He moved sluggishly at first, but even as she turned round and round, jumped up and down in an insanity of fear, he began to stir vigorously. She saw him pouring his awful beauty from the basket upon the bed, then she seized the lamp and ran as fast as she could to the kitchen. The wind from the open door blew out the light and the darkness added to her terror. She sped to the darkness of the yard, slamming the door after her before she thought to set down the lamp. She did not feel safe even on the ground, so she climbed up in the hay barn.

There for an hour or more she lay sprawled upon the hay a gibbering wreck.

Finally, she grew quiet, and after that, coherent thought. With this, stalked through her a cold, bloody rage. Hours of this. A period of introspection, a space of retrospection, then a mixture of both. Out of this an awful calm.

"Well, Ah done de bes' Ah could. If things aint right, Gawd knows taint mah fault."

She went to sleep—a twitchy sleep—and woke up to a faint gray sky. There was a loud hollow sound below. She peered out. Sykes was at the wood-pile, demolishing a wire-covered box.

He hurried to the kitchen door, but hung outside there some minutes before he entered, and stood some minutes more inside before he closed it after him.

The gray in the sky was spreading. Delia descended without fear now, and crouched beneath the low bedroom window. The drawn shade shut out the dawn, shut in the night. But the thin walls held back no sound.

"Dat ol' scratch is woke up now!" She mused at the tremendous whirr inside, which every woodsman knows, is one of the sound illusions. The rattler is a ventriloquist. His whirr sounds to the right, to the left, straight ahead, behind, close under foot—everywhere but where it is. Woe to him who guesses wrong unless he is prepared to hold up his end of the argument! Sometimes he strikes without rattling at all.

Inside, Sykes heard nothing until he knocked a pot lid off the stove while trying to reach the match safe in the dark. He had emptied his pockets at Bertha's.

The snake seemed to wake up under the stove and Sykes made a quick leap into the bedroom. In spite of the gin he had had, his head was clearing now.

"'Mah Gawd!" he chattered, "ef Ah could on'y strack uh light!"

The rattling ceased for a moment as he stood paralyzed. He waited. It seemed that the snake waited also.

"Oh, fuh de light! Ah thought he'd be too sick"—Sykes was muttering to himself when the whirr began again, closer, right underfoot this time. Long before this, Sykes' ability to think had been flattened down to primitive instinct and he leaped—onto the bed.

Outside Delia heard a cry that might have come from a maddened chimpanzee, a stricken gorilla. All the terror, all the horror, all the rage that man possibly could express, without a recognizable human sound.

A tremendous stir inside there, another series of animal screams, the intermittent whirr of the reptile. The shade torn violently down from the window, letting in the red dawn, a huge brown hand seizing the window stick, great dull blows upon the wooden floor punctuating the gibberish of sound long after the rattle of the snake had abruptly subsided. All this Delia could see and hear from her place beneath the window, and it made her ill. She crept over to the four-o'clocks and stretched herself on the cool earth to recover.

She lay there. "Delia. Delia!" She could hear Sykes calling in a most despairing tone as one who expected no answer. The sun crept on up, and he called. Delia could not move—her legs were gone flabby. She never moved, he called, and the sun kept rising.

"Mah Gawd!" She heard him moan, "Mah Gawd fum Heben!" She heard him stumbling about and got up from her flower-bed. The sun was growing warm. As she approached the door she heard him call out hopefully, "Delia, is dat you Ah heah?"

She saw him on his hands and knees as soon as she reached the door. He crept an inch or two toward her—all that he was able, and she saw his horribly swollen neck and his one open eye shining with hope. A surge of pity too strong to support bore her away from that eye that must, could not, fail to see the tubs. He would see the lamp. Orlando with its doctors was too far. She could scarcely reach the Chinaberry tree, where she waited in the growing heat while inside she knew the cold river was creeping up and up to extinguish that eye which must know by now that she knew.

SANCTUARY[1]

Nella Larsen

ON THE SOUTHERN coast, between Merton and Shawboro, there is a strip of desolation some half a mile wide and nearly ten miles long between the sea and old fields of ruined plantations. Skirting the edge of this narrow jungle is a partly grown-over road which still shows traces of furrows made by the wheels of wagons that have long since rotted away or been cut into firewood. This road is little used, now that the state has built its new highway a bit to the west and wagons are less numerous than automobiles.

In the forsaken road a man was walking swiftly. But in spite of his hurry, at every step he set down his feet with infinite care, for the night was windless and the heavy silence intensified each sound; even the breaking of a twig could be plainly heard and the man had need of caution as well as haste.

Before a lonely cottage that shrank timidly back from the road the man hesitated a moment, then struck out across the patch of green in front of it. Stepping behind a clump of bushes close to the house, he looked in through the lighted window at Annie Poole, standing at her kitchen table mixing the supper biscuits.

He was a big, black man with pale brown eyes in which there was an odd mixture of fear and amazement. The light showed streaks of gray soil on his heavy, sweating face and great hands, and on his torn clothes. In his woolly hair clung bits of dried leaves and dead grass.

He made a gesture as if to tap on the window, but turned away

---

1   First published in: *The Forum* 1930: Volume 83, Issue 1.

to the door instead. Without knocking he opened it and went in.

II

The woman's brown gaze was immediately on him, though she did not move. She said, "You ain't in no hurry, is you, Jim Hammer?" It wasn't, however, entirely a question.

"Ah's in trubble, Mis' Poole," the man explained, his voice shaking, his fingers twitching.

"W'at you done now?"

"Shot a man, Mis' Poole."

"Trufe?" The woman seemed calm. But the word was spat out.

"Yas'm. Shot 'im." In the man's tone was something of wonder, as if he himself could not quite believe that he had really done this thing which he affirmed.

"Daid?"

"Dunno, Mis' Poole. Dunno."

"White man o' niggah?"

"Cain't say, Mis' Poole. White man, Ah reckons."

Annie Poole looked at him with cold contempt. She was a tiny, withered woman—fifty perhaps—with a wrinkled face the color of old copper, framed by a crinkly mass of white hair. But about her small figure was some quality of hardness that belied her appearance of frailty. At last she spoke, boring her sharp little eyes into those of the anxious creature before her.

"An' w'at am you lookin' foh me to do 'bout et?"

"Jes' lemme stop till dey's gone by. Hide me till dey passes. Reckon dey ain't fur off now." His begging voice changed to a frightened whimper. "Foh de Lawd's sake, Mis' Poole, lemme stop."

And why, the woman inquired caustically, should she run the dangerous risk of hiding him?

"Obadiah, he'd lemme stop ef he was to home," the man whined.

Annie Poole sighed. "Yas," she admitted slowly, reluctantly, "Ah spec' he would. Obadiah, he's too good to you all no 'count trash." Her slight shoulders lifted in a hopeless shrug. "Yas, Ah reckon he'd do et. Emspecial' seein' how he allus set such a heap o' store by you. Cain't see w'at foh, mahse'f. Ah shuah don' see nuffin' in you but a heap o' dirt."

But a look of irony, of cunning, of complicity passed over her face. She went on, "Still, 'siderin' all an' all, how Obadiah's right fon' o'you, an' how white folks is white folks, Ah'm a-gwine hide you dis one time."

Crossing the kitchen, she opened a door leading into a small bedroom, saying, "Git yo'se'f in dat dere feather bald an'Ah'm a-gwine put de clo's on de top. Don' reckon dey'll fin' you ef dey does look foh you in mah house. An Ah don' spec' dey'll go foh to do cat. Not lessen you been keerless an' let 'em smell you out gittin' hyah." She turned on him a withering look. "But you allus been triflin'. Cain't do nuffin' propah. An' Ah'm a-tellin' you ef dey warn's white folks an'you a po'niggah, Ah shuah wouldn't be lettin' you mess up mah feather bald dis ebenin', 'cose Ah jes' plain con' went you hyah. Ah done kep'mahse'f outen bubble all mah life. So's Obadiah."

"Ah's powahful 'bliged to you, Mis' Poole. You shuah am one good 'omen. De Lawd'll mos' suttinly—"

Annie Poole cut him off. "Dis ain't no time foh all dat kin' o' fiddle-de-roll. Ah does mah duty as Ah sees et 'shout no thanks from you. Ef de Lawd had gib you a white face 'stead o' dat dere black one, Ah shuah would turn you out. Now hush yo' mouf an' git yo'se'f in. An' don' git movin' and scrunchin' undah dose covahs and git yo'se'f kotched in mah house."

Without further comment the man did as he was told. After he had laid his soiled body and grimy garments between her snowy sheets, Annie Poole carefully rearranged the covering and placed piles of freshly laundered linen on top. Then she gave a pat here and there, eyed the result, and, finding it satisfactory, went back to her cooking.

III

Jim Hammer settled down to the racking business of waiting until
the approaching danger should have passed him by. Soon savory
odors seeped in to him and he realized that he was hungry. He
wished that Annie Poole would bring him something to eat. Just
one biscuit. But she wouldn't, he knew. Not she. She was a hard one,
Obadiah's mother.

By and by he fell into a sleep from which he was dragged back by
the rumbling sounds of wheels in the road outside. For a second fear
clutched so tightly at him that he almost leaped from the suffocating
shelter of the bed in order to make some active attempt to escape
the horror that his capture meant. There was a spasm at his heart, a
pain so sharp, so slashing, that he had to suppress an impulse to cry
out. He felt himself falling. Down, down, down…Everything grew
dim and very distant in his memory…Vanished…Came rushing
back.

Outside there was silence. He strained his ears. Nothing. No
footsteps. No voices. They had gone on then. Gone without even
stopping to ask Annie Poole if she had seen him pass that way. A
sigh of relief slipped from him. His thick lips curled in an ugly,
cunning smile. It had been smart of him to think of coming to
Obadiah's mother's to hide. She was an old demon, but he was safe
in her house.

He lay a short while longer, listening intently, and, hearing nothing, started to get up. But immediately he stopped, his yellow eyes
glowing like pale flames. He had heard the unmistakable sound of
men coming toward the house. Swiftly he slid back into the heavy,
hot stuffiness of the bed and lay listening fearfully.

The terrifying sounds drew nearer. Slowly. Heavily. Just for a
moment he thought they were not coming in—they took so long.
But there was a light knock and the noise of a door being opened.
His whole body went taut. His feet felt frozen, his hands clammy,

his tongue like a weighted, dying thing. His pounding heart made it hard for his straining ears to hear what they were saying out there.

"Evenin', Mistah Lowndes." Annie Poole's voice sounded as it always did, sharp and dry. There was no answer. Or had he missed it? With slow care he shifted his position, bringing his head nearer the edge of the bed. Still he heard nothing. What were they waiting for? Why didn't they ask about him?

Annie Poole, it seemed, was of the same mind. "Ah don' reckon youall done traipsed way out hyah jes' foh yo' healf," she hinted.

"There's bad news for you, Annie, I'm 'fraid." The sheriff's voice was low and queer.

Jim Hammer visualized him standing out there—a tall, stooped man, his white tobacco-stained mustache drooping limply at the ends, his nose hooked and sharp, his eyes blue and cold. Bill Lowndes was a hard one too. And white.

"W'atall bad news, Mistah Lowndes?" The woman put the question quietly, directly.

"Obadiah—" the sheriff began—hesitated—began again. "Obadiah—ah—er—he's outside, Annie. I'm 'fraid—"

"Shucks! You done missed. Obadiah, he ain't done nuffin', Mistah Lowndes. Obadiah!" she called stridently, "Obadiah! git hyah an' splain yo'se'f."

But Obadiah didn't answer, didn't come in.

Other men came in. Came in with steps that dragged and halted. No one spoke. Not even Annie Poole. Something was laid carefully upon the floor.

"Obadiah, chile," his mother said softly, "Obadiah, chile." Then, with sudden alarm, "He ain't daid, is he? Mistah Lowndes! Obadiah, he ain't daid?"

Jim Hammer didn't catch the answer to that pleading question. A new fear was stealing over him.

"There was a to-do, Annie," Bill Lowndes explained gently, "at the garage back o' the factory. Fellow tryin' to steal tires. Obadiah heerd a noise an' run out with two or three others. Scared the rascal all right. Fired off his gun an' run. We allow et to be Jim Hammer. Picked up his cap back there. Never was no 'count. Thievin' an' sly. But we'll git 'im, Annie. We'll git 'im."

The man huddled in the feather bed prayed silently. "Oh, Lawd! Ah didn't go to do et. Not Obadiah, Lawd. You knows dat. You knows et." And into his frenzied brain came the thought that it would be better for him to get up and go out to them before Annie Poole gave him away. For he was lost now. With all his great strength he tried to get himself out of the bed. But he couldn't.

"Oh, Lawd! " he moaned. "Oh, Lawd! " His thoughts were bitter and they ran through his mind like panic. He knew that it had come to pass as it said somewhere in the Bible about the wicked. The Lord had stretched out his hand and smitten him. He was paralyzed. He couldn't move hand or foot. He moaned again. It was all there was left for him to do. For in the terror of this new calamity that had come upon him he had forgotten the waiting danger which was so near out there in the kitchen.

His hunters, however, didn't hear him. Bill Lowndes was saying, "We been a- lookin' for Jim out along the old road. Figured he'd make tracks for Shawboro. You ain't noticed anybody pass this evenin', Annie?"

The reply came promptly, unwaveringly. "No, Ah ain't sees nobody pass. Not yet."

IV

Jim Hammer caught his breath.

"Well," the sheriff concluded, "we'll be gittin' along. Obadiah was a mighty fine boy. Ef they was all like him—I'm sorry, Annie. Anything I c'n do, let me know."

"Thank you, Mistah Lowndes."

With the sound of the door closing on the departing men, power to move came back to the man in the bedroom. He pushed his dirt-caked feet out from the covers and rose up, but crouched down again. He wasn't cold now, but hot all over and burning. Almost he wished that Bill Lowndes and his men had taken him with them.

Annie Poole had come into the room.

It seemed a long time before Obadiah's mother spoke. When she did there were no tears, no reproaches; but there was a raging fury in her voice as she lashed out, "Git outer mah feather baid, Jim Hammer, an' outen mah house, an' don' nevah stop thankin' yo' Jesus he done gib you dat black face.

AUTHOR BIOGRAPHIES

DJUNA BARNES

Djuna Barnes (1892–1982) was an American poet, visual artist, journalist, playwright, and novelist. Born in Cornwall-on-Hudson in New York State, Barnes was the granddaughter of the suffragette Zadel Barnes Gustafson, who was herself a successful writer and journalist and was known to have hosted a literary salon during her time in London. Barnes came to be a major figure of, first, the literary world of 1910s Greenwich Village in New York, and later, 1920s and '30s Paris.

Barnes is best known for her novel *Nightwood* (1936), which acquired a cult status as an iconic work of modernist and lesbian fiction during her lifetime. The American edition included an introduction by T. S. Eliot. After initially being rejected by several publishers, the poet and novelist Emily Coleman, who had offered critiques and revisions on early drafts of *Nightwood* and appreciated the novel, had encouraged Eliot to read it, which eventually led Faber and Faber to publish it.

One of the earliest widely read novels to represent female homosexuality and lesbian relationships, *Nightwood* follows the life of Robin Vote, a European woman who leaves an unfulfilling marriage with Felix Volkbein, a man pretending to be an Austrian baron, and travels to America, where she falls in love with another woman, Nora, a publicist for circuses. The two women move back to Paris together, where Nora buys an apartment. Much as she did during her marriage to Volkbein, Robin roams the nights alone, and starts an affair with a widow named Jenny Pentherbridge. The novel concludes with Robin and Jenny moving to New York, with Robin's tendency to go out alone at night returning once again and culminating in Robin's dramatic transformation into a quasi-animalistic form: a creature of the night. The novel employs several modernist techniques, such as its metafictional form, its foregrounding of the medium of language, its self-referentiality, and deliberate subversion of linear narrative.

The story included in this volume, "What Do You See, Madam?" (1916), was first published in the March 27, 1916, issue of *All-Story Cavalier Weekly* and later collected in a volume of Barnes's fiction titled *Smoke and Other Early Stories* (1982). In the setting of a vaudeville show, Barnes's characters explore the limits and opportunities for women who perform and perhaps also embody various female stereotypes to achieve authentic self-expression in a culture thirsting for easy entertainment.

KATE CHOPIN

Kate Chopin (1850–1904; born Katherine O'Flaherty) was a Southern writer of short stories and novels. Born in St. Louis, Missouri, to wealthy parents, she married Oscar Chopin, a French-Creole businessman from Louisiana, in 1870. The couple moved to New Orleans, where Chopin bore six children and fulfilled the duties of the wife of a successful cotton broker. When the family's business failed, they moved to a plantation in Cloutierville, Louisiana. Following her husband's death in 1882, Chopin began to write about communities in the South, in particular Creole and Cajun people. Many of her stories are set in Natchitoches, a north-central region of Louisiana, and were initially published in periodicals in St. Louis and New Orleans, and finally in leading East Coast magazines.

She is most well-known for her shorter fiction, in particular "Désirée's Baby," a story about an interracial child born to the adopted daughter of a French creole family, and "Madame Célestin's Divorce," which is about a French creole woman contemplating divorcing her absent and alcoholic husband. Other well-known stories include "A Respectable Woman" (1894) and "The Storm" (1898), both of which center on a married woman's desire for another man. Chopin's short stories were published in two widely celebrated collections during her lifetime, *Bayou Folk* (1894) and *A Night in Acadie* (1897), and, a half century after her death, in *The Complete Works of Kate Chopin* (1969), when her work was redis-covered and praised for its contemporary sensibility. Chopin's first novel, by contrast, *At Fault* (1890) failed to garner critical acclaim, and her second, *The Awakening* (1899), was castigated for its realis-tic portrayal of a young wife and mother who seeks a life different from that provided by marriage and children.

One of Chopin's principal contributions to the literature of her time is her revision of the dominant Victorian myths and mores about female sexuality and marriage. She partly achieved this through portrayals of women enjoying sex outside of marriage, something considered scandalous in nineteenth-century America. Similarly, in short fiction such as "The Story of an Hour" (1894), Chopin celebrates the autonomy and independence of widows and single women. The story was initially rejected by several publica-tions, but after the success of Chopin's collection *Bayou Folk* in 1894, *Vogue* magazine accepted it as a resubmission with the soft-ened title "The Dream of an Hour." In that story (which perhaps echoes Chopin's memories of her father's death in the collapse, in 1855 when Chopin was five years old, of a railroad bridge connect-ing St. Louis and Jefferson City, Missouri, during the bridge's cer-emonial opening), the protagonist Mrs. Mallard, instead of being totally distraught by her husband's death, marks and feels the grief of his passing, but simultaneously celebrates the many years ahead "that would belong to her absolutely." Even as Chopin would not have called herself a suffragist or a champion of women's rights, her fiction paid close, careful attention to the lives and subjectivities of the women of her time.

SUI SIN FAR/MAUDE EATON

Sui Sin Far (水仙花; 1865–1914) was born Edith Maude Eaton in 1865 to a British father and Chinese mother who immigrated with their children from England, first to the United States and then to Montreal, Canada, in 1872. She grew up in Montreal and worked as a stenographer, typist, and freelance journalist who published articles on the local laws and practices that limited the civil rights and social standing of Chinese Canadians and Chinese Americans. Many Chinese Canadians and Chinese Americans contacted her to ask her to write about difficulties created by racist laws and attitudes. Although she could have "passed" for a white woman under her Western name, she adopted the Cantonese name Sui Sin Far (narcissus flower) and, during this time of intense Sinophobia, she chose to align herself with Chinese Americans. After working as a journalist in the British colony of Jamaica, Sui Sin Far moved for health reasons in 1898 to the United States, where she settled first in San Francisco and then in Seattle's small but growing Chinatown. Sui Sin Far died in 1914 in Montreal.

With her stories, many of which feature Chinese American characters grappling with assimilation, cultural differences, and social conditions, she becomes one of the first authors to present a positive image of Chinese American life for general readers. She is considered the first Asian American author to publish fiction in America. But her stories are more than social commentary about the increasingly hostile attitudes toward Asians and the racist laws affecting them, including the Chinese Exclusion Act of 1882, renewed in 1902, which barred Asian immigration into the United States. Additional laws and ordinances during the following decades restricted not only immigration but also Asian Americans' rights in the country. Her sense of irony, deft character descriptions, and dynamic dialogue in situations specific to the Asian American and Asian Canadian communities render moral dilemmas with universal resonance. The stories achieve a level of authenticity missing from most writings about the Chinese American communities of the time.

Of her stories, "Mrs. Spring Fragrance" is Sui Sin Far's best-known publication. The witty and compelling protagonist is a woman with her own mind who cleverly navigates the political injustices facing Chinese Americans as well as the emotional terrain of her own life. The stories first appeared in 1909 and 1910, and then in a 1912 collection, *Mrs. Spring Fragrance*, lauded in a *New York Times* review: "Miss Eaton has struck a new note in American fiction."

Charlotte Perkins Gilman

Charlotte Perkins Gilman (1860–1935; also known by her first married name, Perkins Stetson) was an American novelist and short story writer. Born in Hartford, Connecticut, Gilman has come to be best known for her short story "The Yellow Wallpaper" (1892), which was first published in *The New England Magazine*. The story is an epistolary fiction that is regarded as an important allegory of the treatment and oppression of women by the Western medical establishment and patriarchal society and at the hands of men who claim to love and care for them.

Comprised of diary entries by a woman diagnosed by her physician husband to be suffering from postpartum "temporary nervous depression," the story uses the conventions of the gothic horror story to account for a woman's experience at the hands of a man who claims to care for her. Though the protagonist initially explains away her confinement in a run-down former nursery in a colonial-style house her husband has leased for the summer, she begins to perceive the figure of a woman on all fours confined behind the yellow wallpaper of her dilapidated room. In an attempt to free the woman, she tears the wallpaper off the nursery walls. However, when her husband arrives, he finds her crawling through the room on all fours, not unlike the woman in the yellow wallpaper, whom the narrator believes she has become.

The narrator's mental descent has been interpreted as Gilman's protest against the social oppression of women and the treatment of women by a largely male medical profession. Gilman, when she sought treatment for lifelong melancholy and "nervous prostration" (conditions that would likely be diagnosed as depression today), was herself prescribed a "rest cure" by the physician Silas Weir Mitchell in Philadelphia, which entailed extensive bed rest and served as the model for the confinement imposed on the narrator of "The Yellow Wallpaper." Gilman was eventually proven right in her rejection of the pseudoscientific "rest cure" when Mary Putnam Jacobi, one of the first female doctors and a suffragist, prescribed her a regimen of mental and physical activity, which was a more effective remedy.

Over the course of her life, Gilman became a prominent women's rights activist and eventually a successful lecturer, earning her living through speaking engagements throughout the United States. Gilman's lectures began to be reported in newspapers and other publications, including *The New York Times*, *The Boston Post*, the *San Francisco Examiner*, and *Woman's Journal*. After relocating to San Francisco in 1894, Gilman served as editor for a weekly publication of the Pacific Coast Women's Press Association, *The Impress* (originally *The Bulletin*). In 1898, Gilman published a widely discussed manifesto titled *Women and Economics* in which she called for "restoring women to economic independence," which would "result in clarifying and harmonizing the human soul." She was inducted into the National Women's Hall of Fame.

FRANCES ELLEN WATKINS HARPER

Frances Ellen Watkins Harper (1825–1911) was born in Baltimore as the only child of free African American parents but raised by an aunt and uncle, Harriet and William Watkins, after her mother died when she was three years old. She attended the Baltimore Academy for Negro Youth, a school run by her uncle, until the age of 13, and then worked in a Quaker household, where she had access to a wide range of literature. After teaching in Ohio and Pennsylvania, she became a traveling speaker for the abolitionist cause. In 1860 she married Fenton Harper, already father to three children of his own, and together they had a daughter. After her husband's death in 1864, Harper continued to support her family through speaking engagements. She was superintendent of the Colored Section of the Philadelphia and Pennsylvania Women's Christian Temperance Union, a member of the American Women's Suffrage Association, and director of the American Association of Colored Youth. As a lecturer and author, Harper was a nineteenth-century household name alongside luminaries such as Elizabeth Cady Stanton and Frederick Douglass, with whom she debated while advocating for Black women's right to vote. Today she is celebrated as one of the key authors and activists of her time. Not only was she the first African American woman known to publish a short story, but as an influential abolitionist, suffragist, author and journalist she co-founded the National Association of Colored Women's Clubs.

A prolific author, Harper published many collections of poetry, several of which were enormously popular. She also published at least four novels, including *Iola Leroy* (1892), essays, and articles. Her short story "The Two Offers" was published in two installments in 1859 in the newly founded *Anglo-African* magazine and is considered the first short story in English published by an African American woman in the United States. "The Two Offers" presents two female cousins deliberating on a marriage proposal at a time when marriage could mean escape from poverty or the beginning of another type of dependency, and not getting married could condemn a woman to penury and misery. The story examines the possibility of women's independence at a time when the idea of marriage as a woman's only economic salvation was challenged by new professional opportunities for women.

"The Two Offers" does not address the abolition of slavery, freedom, or political rights, which Harper addressed in many other speeches and publications. The story does not indicate the main figure's racial identity at all, though first readers who encountered the story in a publication aimed principally at African American readers would probably have assumed it. Harper's lectures and other writings that explicitly address race constitute one dimension of her interventions into American politics and society; her fiction and poetry—no less political—testify to her literary prowess and the audacity of her imagination, and constitute an intervention of a different kind.

ZORA NEALE HURSTON

Zora Hurston (1891–1960) was born in Notasulga, Alabama, on January 15, 1891, to parents who had been enslaved before the Civil War. When Hurston was still young, the family moved to Eatonville, Florida, an African American town where they flourished and Hurston's father became mayor. In 1917, Hurston enrolled at Morgan College, where she also completed her high school degree. She started publishing short stories in 1920 and attended Howard University in Washington, D.C. In 1925 received a scholarship to Barnard College, in New York City, where she graduated in 1928 with a B.A. degree in anthropology. While living in New York City, Hurston befriended writers such as Langston Hughes and Countee Cullen, all of whom participated in and contributed to the explosive cultural scene known today as the Harlem Renaissance.

Hurston returned as an anthropologist to Florida and other Southern states to study and record African American folklore, especially storytelling, songs, and other kinds of cultural expression.

She also traveled to Haiti and Jamaica to study and record religious practice and rituals in the African diaspora communities; her ethnographic findings were published in 1938 as *Tell My Horse: Voodoo and Life in Haiti and Jamaica.*

In 1934, she founded the school of dramatic arts at Bethune-Cookman College, in Florida, and also worked as a drama teacher at the North Carolina College for Negroes at Durham. Although a prolific writer, journalist, scholar, filmmaker, and teacher, Hurston was not adequately compensated for her work and had to enter the St. Lucie County Welfare Home as she was unable to take care of herself. Hurston died of heart disease on January 28, 1960, in relative obscurity, considering her pivotal status in American letters during the 1920s and 1930s.

In her novels, short stories, and plays Hurston often depicted African American life in the South. For her stories, she often drew on her ethnographic studies, which included extensive interviews and recordings. Hurston was a prominent figure in the New York cultural scene who dedicated her life and work to promoting and studying black culture.

Her works include the novels, *Jonah's Gourd Vine* (1934), *Their Eyes were Watching God* (1937), *Moses, Man of the Mountain* (1939); a play, *Mule Bone: A Comedy of Negro Life*, co-written in 1930 with Langston Hughes; a literary anthology on African-American folklore in Florida, *Mules and Men* (1935); her autobiography *Dust Tracks on a Road* (1942); and several posthumous publications, including the nonfiction book, *Barracoon: The Story of the Last "Black Cargo"* (2018). Today Hurston's works are available in expertly edited editions which include stories and poems not republished during her lifetime.

Unfortunately, some of Hurston's greatest work was ignored by parts of the mainstream literary audience, meaning mostly the white literary and publishing world, soon after its original publication in the 1930s. However, she gained a following among

African Americans, and in 1975 rose again to wider prominence after novelist Alice Walker published an article about her lasting significance. Today Hurston's novels are considered a staple in the American canon, and the wider range of her publications generates superb commentary and criticism.

NELLA LARSEN

Nellallitea "Nella" Larsen (1891–1964) was a novelist of the Harlem Renaissance, a period in the early twentieth century marked by the flourishing of African American artists, writers, musicians, and performers in Harlem, New York. The author of two novels, *Quicksand* (1928) and *Passing* (1929), Larsen gained a reputation as one of the most prominent writers of the Harlem Renaissance. However, from the late 1930s until the mid-1980s, Larsen's work passed over into relative obscurity and her novels languished out of print until they were republished by the scholar Deborah E. McDowell in 1986.

Larsen was born on the South Side of Chicago into a mixed-race family, her father an Afro-Caribbean man from the Danish West Indies and her mother an immigrant from Denmark. Her background plays a part in the novel she is best known for, *Passing*, a psychologically discerning tale of two light-skinned Black women from the same background who end up in very different circumstances based on their personal decisions about what racial group to belong to. When they meet later in life, the budding friendship has devastating consequences.

In addition to her two novels, Larsen also wrote a number of short stories, including "The Wrong Man" (1926), "Freedom" (1926), and "Sanctuary" (1930). The last of these was written in response to or adapted from the English writer Sheila Kaye-Smith's short story "Mrs. Adis" (1922). Larsen's writing of "Sanctuary" led her to be accused of plagiarism in a destructive public controversy, which damaged her career and probably caused her to not publish anything afterwards. Whereas it was seen as plagiarism at the time, Larsen's story is more accurately described as an adaptation, which transposed the struggles of the British working class depicted in Kaye-Smith's "Mrs. Adis" into the specific situation of white supremacy and class oppression at work in the American South. The scholar Kelli Larson argues that this mode of adaptation was common in African American theater of the period, and Nella Larsen was not an outlier in her adaptation of Kaye-Smith's story.

GERTRUDE STEIN

Gertrude Stein (1874–1946) was born in Allegheny, Pennsylvania, and lived in numerous places in the United States and Europe before settling permanently in Paris in 1903. She always identified strongly as an American, and produced a great number of works in many different genres, most of them characterized by a fearless ethos of experimentation, often resulting in unexpected phrasings, words, and syntax, executed with great discipline. A major American modernist writer, poet, playwright, and art collector, Stein convened a literary salon in Paris with her partner, Alice B. Toklas, which included such luminaries as Ernest Hemingway, Ezra Pound, F. Scott Fitzgerald, Sinclair Lewis, Henri Matisse, and Pablo Picasso. As one of the first highly visible and a publicly identified lesbian artists, her first best seller was an autobiography written in the voice of her partner and paradoxically titled *The Autobiography of Alice B. Toklas* (1932).

Among Stein's more well-known books are: her posthumously published first novel, *Q.E.D.* (written in 1903), which describes a romantic affair between Stein and her friends Mabel Haynes, Grace Lounsbury, and Mary Bookstaver during their time at Johns Hopkins University in Baltimore; *Three Lives* (1909), a collection of three stories, "The Good Anna," "Melanctha," and "The Gentle Lena," which was Stein's first critical success; and *The Making of*

Americans (1925), a story of two families, the Herslands and the Dehnings, which is emblematic of several modernist methods employed by Stein, including metafictional reflections on the writing process, the use of the present participle, heavy use of repetition, a restricted vocabulary, and the lack of chapters to divide up the story.

The story included in this volume, "Miss Furr and Miss Skeene" (written in 1910–11), involved two women, Helen Furr and Georgine Skeene, who choose to live together. While innocent enough on the surface, the story activates the double entendre of the word "gay," more readily apparent to today's readers than to those in Stein's day, to render a positive representation of a lesbian relationship. The story was originally published in a collection of Stein's stories titled *Geography and Plays* (1922).

Stein was a literary giant of her time, collaborating with some of the most prominent and celebrated artists and writers of the period. Two quotations by Stein are now idiomatic expressions in the English language, namely "Rose is a rose is a rose is a rose," and "there is no there there," the latter from a memoir, *Everybody's Autobiography* (1937). Stein's political views, however, were fraught. While some scholars emphasize her pro-immigration, feminist, and democratic politics within the United States, Stein criticized Franklin D. Roosevelt and the New Deal. And during her time in Paris, she publicly endorsed the Spanish fascist General Francisco Franco and expressed some admiration for the pro-Nazi leader of the French Vichy regime, Marshal Philippe Pétain. Stein died on July 27, 1946, in Paris. Both Stein and her partner Alice B. Toklas are buried next to one another in the Cimetière du Père-Lachaise in Paris.

Elizabeth Drew Stoddard

Elizabeth Drew Stoddard (1823–1902) was a prolific writer of poetry and fiction. Born in Mattapoisett, Massachusetts, Stoddard attended several boarding schools before studying at Wheaton Female Seminary in the town of Norton, Massachusetts. After her marriage to the poet Richard Henry Stoddard, the couple moved to New York City in 1852, where Elizabeth became a fixture in the city's literary and artistic scenes. While Stoddard always showed an interest in literature, her move to New York marked the beginning of her literary career. Her poetry was published in many of the leading magazines of the time, including *Harper's Bazaar*, *Harper's Monthly*, and *The Atlantic Monthly*.

Stoddard is today most widely known for her novel *The Morgesons* (1862), the first of her three novels, the other two being *Two Men* (1865) and *Temple House* (1867). *The Morgesons* is a bildungsroman with a female protagonist, Cassandra Morgeson, and follows her from her teenage years into young adulthood as she passes through various stages of intellectual development. Unlike most domestic fiction of the time, which was told by an omniscient narrator, the novel is narrated by Cassandra herself in the first person. The novel places less importance on standard features in domestic fiction, such as amusing character descriptions and dramatic action, and instead focuses on Cassandra's interiority, thoughts, and observations, marking a broader psychological shift in fiction that would see its apotheosis in literary modernism and stream-of-consciousness writing over half a century later. Unlike some of her literary predecessors among American women writers, Stoddard largely foregoes sentimentality in favor of detailed character development, psychological depth, and irony.

Aside from being a vivid sketch of a dysfunctional family, *The Morgesons* is a powerful indictment of oppressive patriarchal norms and structures that American women were forced to navigate in the nineteenth century. *The Morgesons* received critical acclaim during Stoddard's lifetime and was favorably compared with the fiction of other famed writers of the period, including Charlotte, Emily, and Anne Brontë, Nathaniel Hawthorne, and Honoré de Balzac, even as

Stoddard attracted the critical ire of none other than Henry James, who penned a disapproving review of her novel *Two Men*.

Edith Wharton

Edith Wharton (1862–1937) was an American novelist and short story writer known for her literary depictions of the late nineteenth-century American "Gilded Age" and turn-of-the-century Europe. Born Edith Newbold Jones to an affluent family on Manhattan's West 23rd Street in 1862, Wharton spent a large part of her childhood in Italy, Germany, and France. After her return to New York in 1872, Wharton's parents arranged for her to receive lessons from a governess, Anna Catherine Bahlmann. It is from this point on that Wharton's literary career begins with her first collection of poems, *Verses* (1878), appearing six years later.

In 1885, at the age of twenty-three, Wharton married Edward "Teddy" Robbins Wharton, a sportsman and socialite who suffered from acute depression. In 1897, the couple purchased and moved into an apartment on Park Avenue and 79th Street, where they lived for the early years of their marriage. The marriage was strained for many years. Wharton finally moved to France in 1911 and divorced Teddy two years later. She eventually died in France in 1937, before the onset of World War II, and is buried in the Cimetière des Gonards in Versailles.

In 1905, Wharton published her novel *The House of Mirth*, to great acclaim. She published additional novels or novellas which were equally celebrated: *Ethan Frome* (1911), *The Reef* (1912), *The Custom of the Country* (1913), *Summer* (1917), and *The Age of Innocence* (1920). Wharton is particularly admired for her short fiction, some of which was collected in *The Descent of Man and Other Stories* (1904). A masterful stylist and highly entertaining writer, Wharton's novels share a feminist and acute knowledge of both the human heart and the spoken and unspoken rules of society.

Wharton's story "The Reckoning" (1902) examines what the freedom to choose would mean in a marriage where both partners vow to respect the other's choices. It was published at a moment when divorce was still considered a failure, rather than an option for most people, and when women gained economic independence in far greater numbers than before. Published in *Harper's Monthly Magazine*, "The Reckoning" follows the protagonist Julia Westall, who has left her rich first husband, John Armant, for a less wealthy man, Clement Westall. When Julia and Clement decide to get together, they agree that they will leave the other free to move on if either of them ceases to love the other. However, Julia faces a crisis when Clement, after ten years with Julia, appears to want to leave.

Wharton is remembered as a major writer of short fiction, a brilliant and incisive commentator on American society, and also an originator of literature committed to authentic representation of female characters. While many of her works describe the specific situation of mostly upper-class life in Europe and North America, many of them have broader implication about the transition of society and especially gender relations in the wake of the industrial revolution, urbanization, and the wholesale transformation of Western society in the early twentieth century.

www.ingramcontent.com/pod-product-compliance
Lightning Source LLC
Chambersburg PA
CBHW032014170626
46807CB00006B/2808